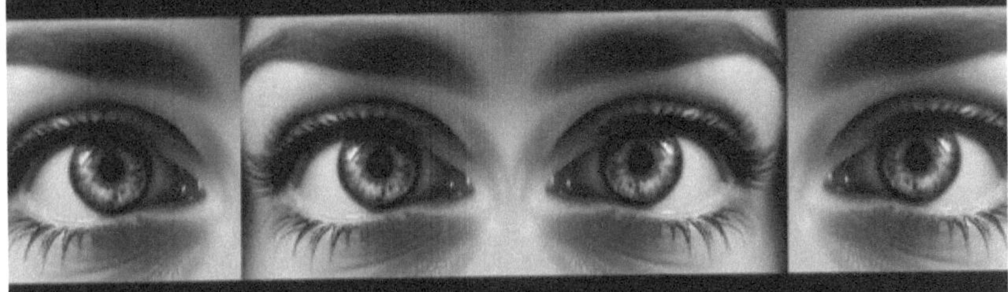

OBSESSION
UNLEASHED
CS RAJU

Obsession Unleashed

CSRaju

Published by CSRaju, 2023.

This is a work of fiction. Similarities to real people, places, or events are entirely coincidental.

OBSESSION UNLEASHED

First edition. September 16, 2023.

Copyright © 2023 CSRaju.

ISBN: 979-8223223733

Written by CSRaju.

Author's Words......

For all those who venture into the depths of this novel - your engagement fuels my creativity. Thanks to my son Krishna Vasanth who supported me in this hard road ahead. May this story challenge your thoughts and captivate your imagination.

OBSESSION UNLEASHED

Chapter 1.

Teena's apartment was not just a living space but a sanctuary for her artistic soul. Situated in the heart of New York City's bustling arts district, it was a haven filled with an eclectic mix of colors, textures, and a testament to her endless creativity. Canvases of all sizes leaned against walls, some completed with masterful strokes, others waiting for her inspiration to breathe life into them.

As she stood before her easel, her fingers caressing the paintbrush with grace and precision, Teena's face was illuminated by the natural sunlight filtering through the curtains. Her captivating eyes, the color of rich hazelnut, sparkled with passion as they focused intently on her latest painting—a hauntingly beautiful portrait that seemed to mirror her own deep, complex emotions.

Her brush danced across the canvas, each stroke a symphony of color and form, revealing the depth of her talent and the intensity of her emotions. She seemed lost in a world of her own creation, a serene oasis where time and the chaos of city life stood still.

Teena's whisper broke the silence, soft but resolute, as she admired her nearly completed work. "Just a few more touches and it will be perfect." The painting was more than art to her—it was a piece of her soul, a reflection of emotions too profound for mere words.

Her long, chestnut hair was pulled back into a loose bun, a few stray strands falling gently around her face. Dressed in a simple white shirt splattered with paint and worn jeans, she looked every bit the artist, consumed by her craft.

As she added the final touches, her thoughts drifted to her twin sister, Reena, and how different their lives were despite their striking resemblance. Teena's world was filled with colors and shapes, while Reena's was a landscape of facts and mysteries. Yet they shared a bond that went beyond mere genetics—a connection of minds and hearts that only they could truly understand.

As the day wore on, Teena's mind wandered further, filled with dreams and possibilities. Her heart ached with longing for something she couldn't quite grasp, a mystery that was yet to unfold.

Reena's office in Carmel, a picturesque small town nestled between golden beaches and rolling hills, is more than just a workspace; it's a battlefield of intellect, a shrine to justice, and the nerve center of her relentless pursuit of truth. Stacks of newspapers, files, and handwritten notes clutter the room, each a testament to her mind's untiring commitment to the facts.

Though the outside world is filled with the serenity of waves gently caressing the shore and the distant call of seagulls, Reena Harrison's office is a hive of activity. In her late 20s and the elder twin sister to Teena by mere minutes, Reena sits at her desk, her eyes glued to the computer screen, completely absorbed in her latest investigation.

The walls of the office bear witness to her past triumphs, adorned with newspaper clippings and photographs that track her impressive career. The window frames a view of the tranquil town, but Reena remains cocooned in her world of information, shielded from distraction, committed to her cause.

Her very essence seems to vibrate with relentless energy, an unyielding desire to unearth the hidden, no matter the cost. "Come on, there must be something more," she mutters to herself, her voice filled with fierce determination.

Her eyes, intense and unyielding, scan the screen, each line of data a potential clue. Her fingers dance across the keyboard with a grace that belies their strength, each keystroke a testament to her unwavering resolve.

Reena's relationship with Teena is a cherished part of her identity. Yet, their paths are markedly different. Reena's life is one of aggressive daring, a continuous dance on the edge of danger and intrigue, while her location in Carmel, often associated with peace and beauty, contrasts sharply with the gritty realities she unravels.

Her character, aggressive yet compassionate, daring yet methodical, sets her apart as a formidable force in her field. In a town defined by its scenic beauty and quiet charm, Reena's office stands as a beacon of integrity and determination, an embodiment of conviction in a world often clouded by deceit and her relentless pursuit, a lingering sense of admiration and intrigue for a woman who defies expectations is left behind, her shining brightly against the backdrop of Carmel's idyllic landscape.

The day was as bright and lively as the flashbulbs that ignited the bustling photo studio in the heart of New York city. Filled with the effervescent hum of activity, the studio was a world unto itself, where lights, cameras, and artistry fused into one synchronized dance.

In the center of this creative whirlwind stood John Carter, a ruggedly handsome young man in his mid-20s, his magnetic charm palpable in every corner of the room. His physique was sculpted to perfection, his features undeniable, but it was his eyes that held the room captive. They were windows to something deeper, a complexity that whispered of mysteries yet to be revealed.

Photographers, assistants, and crew members moved around him, their voices blending into a symphony of commands and encouragement. The flashes popped, the shutters clicked, and John, with practiced ease, struck pose after pose.

"That's it, John! Hold that pose. Perfect!" a photographer exclaimed, eyes twinkling with professional satisfaction.

John's smile was humble yet confident, a delightful mix of grace and gratitude. "Thanks, but it's all about the lighting and the lens. You make me look good," he replied, his voice carrying an unpretentious charm.

The shoot continued a dance of lights, angles, and artistry, with John as the central figure, his movements effortless and natural. Each pose revealed another facet of his personality, each clicks a snapshot of his essence. The session moved towards its end, each frame a testament to John's undeniable talent and magnetic presence.

Moments later, in the quiet sanctuary of his dressing room, John sat before the mirror, his face still radiant with the energy of the shoot but now softened by introspection.

He looked at himself, not with the eyes of vanity but with the clear, thoughtful gaze of a man who understood his dreams and the path he needed to walk. "It's not just about the looks; it's about the passion, the drive. I won't stop until I reach the top," he said to himself, his voice tinged with unwavering determination.

In the solitude of his thoughts, John Carter's dreams seemed more tangible, his goals clearer. The reflection in the mirror was not just an image but a symbol of what he aspired to be. A promise to himself, a commitment to excellence, and an understanding that beauty was but a part of the journey. The real essence lay in the heart, the soul, and the unwavering resolve to become more.

Nestled in the heart of New York City, a place known for its unrelenting pace and towering ambitions, lies a park—an oasis of tranquility amidst the concrete jungle. It's a beloved retreat for city dwellers, a spot where skyscrapers meet the sky, and the vibrant energy of the city melds with the gentle calm of nature.

Teena, a woman in her late 20s, both captivating and enigmatic, finds solace in this park, strolling along the winding paths that mirror the complex twists and turns of her own thoughts. The air smells of freshly cut grass mixed with distant hints of city life, a unique blend that is quintessentially New York.

Then, in a moment as fleeting as a heartbeat, a ray of sunlight breaks through the canopy of trees, illuminating a figure near the fountain. The light dances on the water, reflecting the city's dynamism, but it's the man that seizes Teena's attention.

With a grace, standing lost in thought, his charisma blending with a touch of vulnerability. The city's soft hum serves as a backdrop to this unexpected encounter, and Teena's heart skips a beat. Who is he? The question echoes in her mind, a whisper that grows louder with every heartbeat.

There's something about him. A connection, a pull that goes beyond mere physical attraction. Her eyes remain locked on his face, captivated by his grace and allure.

As she inches closer, drawn to him by an inexplicable magnetic force, her surroundings begin to fade. The towering skyscrapers, the distant honks of city traffic, even the iconic landmarks of New York—all of it becomes a faint background to the symphony playing in her heart.

In a city of millions, where anonymity is the norm and connections are often fleeting, Teena finds herself drawn to this stranger. He's like a work of art, unknown and untouchable, yet calling out to her very soul.

She moves closer, her mind racing, her heart fluttering with a mix of excitement and apprehension. The connection feels profound, too intense to be ignored, too real to be merely a figment of her imagination.

In that New York City Park, amidst the bustle of life and the tranquility of nature, two souls meet in a dance orchestrated by fate. It's a beginning, a spark that ignites a connection that transcends the mundane, reaching into the very fabric of destiny.

It's love at first sight in the city that never sleeps, a moment that defies reason, defies explanation, and promises to blossom into something more—a story only they can write, a journey only they can take.

In the heart of New York City, the bustling commercial capital where everyone seems engaged in a relentless race towards success, lies a sanctuary of calm and elegance. Sarah Miller's high-rise apartment is a testament to sophistication, comfort, and the rewards of hard work. With floor-to-ceiling windows that unveil breathtaking views of the skyline, the place exudes an aura of achievement.

But it's not just the cityscape that captivates the senses. The modern decor, carefully chosen, reflects the refined taste of Sarah, a woman in her early 30s, warm, empathetic, and successful in her own right.

On a plush sofa, beneath the soft glow of designer lights, sits Teena, her friend, a woman whose enchanting presence is marked by her late 20s and an aura of mystique. Her mind, however, is not on the opulence surrounding her but on an encounter that has left her captivated, enthralled by emotions she's never felt before.

Sarah, recognizing the starry-eyed look in her friend's eyes, can't help but tease, her voice dancing with curiosity and knowing affection. "Spill the beans, Teena. I can see that look in your eyes. What's got you all starry-eyed?"

Teena blushes, the words tumbling out with a mixture of excitement and nervousness. "I... I saw someone today, Sarah. It's like nothing I've ever felt before. He was standing near the fountain at the park, and... I couldn't take my eyes off him."

The conversation flows a playful banter that reveals not just the excitement of a newfound attraction but also the depth of friendship between these two women. They've been through highs and lows together, their bond strengthened over time, a thick friendship that transcends mere acquaintance.

Sarah teases and reassures in equal measure, her words a mix of humor and wisdom. "Ah, love at first sight, huh? You've finally fallen head over heels, huh, Miss Mysterious? Whoa, slow down there, Sherlock! You might just run into him again at the park. It's a big city, but destiny works in mysterious ways."

The afternoon unfolds into a gentle ebb and flow of conversation, filled with laughter, dreams, and the simple joy of companionship. As the sun dips behind the skyscrapers, casting a golden hue over the city, the two women make plans for a night out, the promise of adventure laced with the underlying excitement of Teena's mystery man.

Sarah's voice, filled with love and encouragement, brings the scene to a close, a poetic reflection of the city itself. "Well, let fate do its thing. In the meantime, how about we plan a fun night out? Take your mind off this mystery man and enjoy the city lights. Who knows, he might just show up when you least expect it." In a city known for its chaos, in a high-rise apartment where success meets style, two friends find solace, understanding, and the thrill of the unknown. Their laughter and shared dreams linger in the air, blending with the enchanting glow of New York City. The connection between Teena and Sarah, the mysterious allure of a stranger, and the promise of what tomorrow may hold create a rich tapestry that resonates long after their conversation ends.

Teena's heart beats with a peculiar rhythm, driven by an unexplained connection to a man whose name she doesn't even know. Her feet move briskly through New York's bustling streets, the city's noise fading into a distant murmur as her mind replays the image of his face. The memory of his eyes, the way the sunlight danced on his skin at the park, haunts her every step.

"I have to find him. I can't let this chance slip away." Her thoughts are a whispered mantra, guiding her relentless search.

Cafes once filled with the scent of coffee and chatter become silent stages of expectation as Teena scans the sea of faces, hoping to glimpse his smile. She questions waiters and patrons, describing him as best as she can, her voice steady but her hands betraying a tremor of anticipation.

The park, where fate first intertwined their paths, calls to her. She sits on a familiar bench, every rustle of leaves or distant laugh prickling her senses. Hours slip by in a tense vigil, but the man she seeks remains elusive.

Across street intersections and bustling squares, Teena's search continues. Flyers with his description flutter from her hands to those of strangers, her eyes pleading for recognition, her voice echoing in the urban cacophony.

Her journey takes her on buses and trains, her gaze sweeping over the cityscape, a canvas of dreams and longing. The city's sprawling beauty becomes a complex puzzle, each piece a potential clue to his whereabouts.

"Where are you?" Her voice breaks, a whisper lost in the wind.

She delves into libraries, pouring over records, newspapers, and directories. The musty smell of books and the soft rustle of pages become her companions in this desperate quest.

Even the boundless realms of the internet yield no answers. Keyboards click and screens flicker, but his image remains confined to her memories.

"Come on, where are you hiding?"

Frustration mounts and despair threatens to creep in. The search is a maze, and she is caught in its twists and turns.

"It's like finding a needle in a haystack."

Yet, Teena's determination doesn't wane. The connection she felt that day in the park was real, profound, something she had never felt before. It's a bond she can't ignore, a destiny she feels compelled to fulfill.

No matter the obstacles, no matter the odds, she won't give up. Her heart knows what it wants, and it won't rest until she finds him.

Her search continues, a testament to faith, hope, and the mysterious workings of love.

Chapter 2.

Teena's stylish yet minimalistic apartment glows with soft, dimmed light, casting a warm hue over her art supplies. The night outside her window is calm, but her mind is anything but. On a video call with her twin sister, Reena, she works on a painting, her calm and composed personality reflected in the cool tones of her surroundings.

"Reena, today I went back to the park where we used to play as kids. It brought back memories," Teena says calmly, painting. Her voice trails off, filled with nostalgia as her eyes glimmer with unspoken emotions.

"That's nice, Teena. I miss those days too. Remember how we used to play pretend and invent secret worlds?" Reena replies warmly from her home, her face lighting up with the memory, a soft smile playing on her lips.

"Mhmm. Those were good times." Teena smiles, hiding a yearning, an ache for those simpler times.

Reena laughs, leaning forward, curiosity piqued. "Well, I can't wait to see what you're working on when it's done."

"If only you knew what I'm really painting, Reena," Teena thinks to herself, her brush hesitating, the image of the unknown man's face lingering in her mind.

"Teena, you mean the world to me. You've always been there for me," Reena says softly, her eyes sincere, filled with genuine affection.

"I'll always be there for you, Reena, even if it means keeping my feelings hidden," Teena thinks, her heart heavy with the secret.

"Is everything okay, Teena? You seem a bit distant," Reena asks, concerned. "I'm fine, sis. Just absorbed in my art, as usual," Teena responds, maintaining composure, but her hands betray a slight tremble.

"Well, keep creating magic with those brushes of yours. And remember, I'm always here for you, no matter what," Reena says, reassuringly.

"I know, Reena. Love you." "Love you too, sis."

They end the call, and Teena stands before the partially painted canvas, her cool exterior masking the longing and confusion within her. Her eyes linger on the incomplete face on the canvas—a face that's haunting her dreams and waking moments.

"I'll keep you hidden, man, just like these feelings," she whispers to herself, a mixture of hope and despair. Her eyes linger on the canvas, her mind a whirlpool of emotion. The love she shares with her sister is unbreakable, but the secret she harbors is a weight she must bear alone. Her brush poised, her heart torn between her love for her twin sister and her pursuit of the unknown man who has captured her soul, Teena stands before the canvas—a testament to her hidden desire. The mystery deepens.

The city street buzzes with the noise of a typical day. Cars honk impatiently, people chatter as they rush past, street vendors call out their wares. Amidst the chaotic symphony of urban life, John walks down the bustling avenue, with a pensive look on his face. His thoughts are miles away from the hustle and bustle surrounding him; he's lost in a world of his own.

He's a tall figure with a soft smile that betrays a gentle soul. Though surrounded by noise, he seems to be wrapped in a cocoon of tranquility. The cares and worries of the city dwellers don't touch him.

Suddenly, his eyes catch a sight that pulls him from his reverie: an old man, his face a roadmap of wrinkles, each one a testament to the years he's lived and the wisdom he's gained. The Old Man is struggling, his frail hands trembling under the weight of grocery bags, filled to the brim and threatening to spill.

Without thinking, something inside John propels him forward. His heart, always guided by empathy and compassion, leads the way.

"Sir, let me help you with that," he says gently, approaching the Old Man, his voice like a soothing balm.

The Old Man looks up, his eyes widening with surprise and gratitude. "Oh, thank you, young man. These bags are heavier than they look."

John's smile grows warmer, his eyes twinkling. "No problem at all. Where are you headed? I can carry them for you."

The Old Man, still surprised by the unexpected kindness, points to a blue house just around the corner. Together, they begin to walk, the Old Man's pace slow but determined, John's steps matching his.

As they walk, the Old Man studies John, curiosity gleaming in his eyes. "You seem different from others around here. You have a kind heart."

John looks down, a touch of modesty in his voice. "I just believe in helping others when I can."

"Kindness is a rare quality these days. I hope you never lose it," the Old Man says, his voice rich with wisdom and experience.

"I hope so too," John replies thoughtfully, a shadow crossing his face, a hint at deeper thoughts and hidden complexities.

They arrive at the blue house, and John carefully sets the bags down by the door. The Old Man's gratitude is palpable, his eyes moist with unshed tears.

"Thank you, my boy. You've made an old man's day a little brighter," he says, his voice cracking.

"It was my pleasure, sir," John grins, his heart full.

He waves goodbye to the Old Man and continues his way, the viewer is left with an indelible impression of his warm and compassionate nature, a bright spark of humanity in a cold, busy world.

Reena's office in Carmel buzzed with intensity as she and her colleagues gathered around, their minds fixed on the cryptocurrency scandal. With her focused gaze, Reena led the conversation, her voice firm, her resolve clear.

"This scandal is just the tip of the iceberg," she stated. "We must get to the bottom of it and expose those responsible."

Her colleagues nodded in agreement, their enthusiasm mirroring hers. "We're with you, Reena," one of them assured her. "The people deserve to know the truth."

While the office was alive with talk and determination, outside on the town's serene streets, Teena made her way toward Reena's office building, a surprise visit dancing in her thoughts, a playful smile on her face. She carried a bag of their favorite childhood snacks, a personal touch to make her sister's day special.

Teena snuck into the building, her excitement growing with every step. Entering

Reena's private office, she placed the snacks on Reena's desk and looked around, her eyes taking in the room, her mind filled with memories.

In the main office, Reena continued to command the situation, directing her assistant, Jane, to gather specific files related to the transactions. Jane left, unknowingly passing Teena in the hallway without recognizing her.

As the day wore on, Reena's office gradually emptied until she was left alone. She glanced at the clock, her stomach growling for a particular snack. Deciding to indulge herself, she headed to her private office, only to find Teena standing there, a grin spreading across her face.

"Teena?!" Reena exclaimed, her surprise turning into pure delight. "Surprise!" Teena replied, her arms open for an embrace.

"What are you doing here?!" Reena laughed, hugging her tightly.

"I just wanted to see my sister in action," Teena confessed, her eyes twinkling. "And I brought our favorite snacks."

They sat down, their serious talk giving way to laughter and shared memories, the pressure of the cryptocurrency investigation momentarily forgotten. They munched on the familiar snacks, each bite taking them back to simpler times.

"I'm proud of you, Reena," Teena said at one point, her voice filled with sincerity.

"Thank you," Reena whispered, her eyes soft. "You know I couldn't do it without you."

Their time together was a rare oasis in their busy lives, a moment where they could be sisters without the weight of their responsibilities. But eventually, they had to part, a silent promise exchanged in their farewell embrace.

Back in her office, Reena's determination was renewed, the love and support from her sister a guiding beacon. The mystery of the cryptocurrency scandal lay ahead, a challenge to conquer, but she knew she was not alone.

Her sister's love and the warmth of their shared memories would always be with her, fueling her strength, and guiding her path. The investigation continued, but now with a touch of home to keep her grounded.

Reena's house was a quaint and artistically adorned space, a small independent house on the beachside. The living room overlooked the serene view of the beach, and few of Teena's paintings hung on the walls, subtle reminders of the artistic bond they shared.

Reena and Teena sat at the dining table, sipping coffee, and engaged in lively conversation. Reena's small-sized Pomeranian dog, Max, lay contentedly at her feet.

"It's been too long since we spent some quality time together, Teena," Reena smiled.

Teena nodded, "I know, Reena. Our busy lives always keep us apart, but we're never truly far from each other."

Reena's eyes landed on Teena's painting. "Your creativity never ceases to amaze me, Teena. The way you put emotions on canvas is unparalleled. Like this painting here, the way you've hidden the imagery behind the brush strokes, it's fascinating."

Teena laughed. "That's the beauty of art, Reena. It allows me to express my inner world without saying a word."

Reena stroked Max, turning serious. "Speaking of inner worlds, my journalism is taking me deeper into some dangerous territories. The corruption, the scandals. But it's thrilling. The pressure to investigate, to expose the truth, it's like being in a battle."

"And you're the brave warrior, fighting fearlessly. I admire your courage, sis. You're making a real difference," Teena said supportively.

Reena playfully responded, "And your paintings are like little pieces of you that I can keep close. They're mysterious, just like you."

"Well, as long as they're with you, they're in the right place," Teena smiled gratefully.

Teena reached down to pet Max. "I must admit, Reena, he's got quite the charm. You sure he hasn't been taking lessons from you?"

Reena pretended to look affronted. "Lessons from me? Are you implying I'm as sneaky as a puppy?"

Teena nodded solemnly, "Exactly that! But don't worry, it's one of the things I love about you."

"Oh really?" Reena smirked. "Well, maybe next time I'll teach him how to paint, and then he can take over your job!"

They both broke into peals of laughter, the sound filling the room.

"Imagine that," Teena gasped between laughs, "Max with a little paintbrush, creating masterpieces!"

"You think it's funny now," Reena playfully warned, "but wait until he becomes more famous than you!"

They laughed again, their shared sense of humor drawing them closer. The joy in the room was palpable, a reflection of their deep connection.

"Whatever happens," Teena said finally, her voice soft but firm, "we'll always be there for each other. Even if Max does become a world-renowned artist."

Reena reached across the table to squeeze her sister's hand. "Always."

The laughter eventually subsided, but the warmth remained, a beautiful testament to the love and understanding that bound the two sisters together.

Reena's bedroom was bathed in the soft glow of daylight, filled with a sense of intimacy that only close sisters could share. The room's décor was simple but elegant, much like Reena herself, with touches that hinted at Teena's artistic influence.

In front of the full-length mirror, Reena and Teena stood side by side, wearing identical outfits. Their reflections were mirror images of each other, each curve and contour matched perfectly, their smiles equally radiant.

"It's remarkable how identical we are," Reena remarked, her eyes dancing with amusement. "Even our body shapes and curves are the same. We're like two masterpieces of art, aren't we?"

Teena's eyes sparkled with intrigue. "Let's put it to the test."

They moved to the wardrobe and, with an air of playfulness, swapped outfits, including undergarments. When they returned to the mirror, they were astounded.

"You know, Teena," Reena said, her voice laced with surprise, "even in each other's clothes, we look almost indistinguishable. It's a celebration of our womanhood, our connection as sisters. Our bodies tell the same story."

Teena nodded; her voice soft with understanding. "It's like we were destined to share everything. Our bodies, our minds, our souls. We're reflections of each other's essence."

After this profound moment, they sat down at their desks with a notebook and a pen.

"How about we test our handwriting strikes?" Reena suggested, her eyes gleaming with curiosity.

"Great idea! Let's write the same sentence and compare," Teena agreed, her excitement infectious.

They paused, thinking about what they should write, their eyes meeting as an idea formed in their minds.

"How about our favorite quote?" Teena suggested.

"Yes, the one that speaks to our hearts," Reena agreed.

They each wrote the sentence, the pen gliding smoothly across the paper: "Two souls with but a single thought, two hearts that beat as one."

When they compared the notes, they were astonished.

"Look at this! Our handwriting strikes are identical," Reena exclaimed, her voice filled with wonder.

"It's like we have the same thoughts flowing through our fingers," Teena replied, her eyes wide with amazement.

They laughed together, a melody that filled the room with warmth. "True. We're like two halves of a whole," Teena said her voice tender.

Their eyes met, and at that moment, they understood each other completely. They were more than just sisters; they were soulmates, connected by an unbreakable bond that transcended physical appearance. In each other's presence, they felt whole, content, and deeply proud of their unique identity.

They shared a warm smile, feeling a deeper connection through these tests of their identicalness. Their laughter continued, echoing through the room, a testament to their love and understanding...

Teena stands nervously in line at the United Friendship Bank's lobby, clutching Reena's identification and a withdrawal slip. The hustle and bustle of the banking floor do nothing to distract her from the task at hand. Beads of sweat form on her brow, and she wipes them away with a trembling hand, subtly trying to press her fingers on various surfaces to leave her fingerprints.

"Just act like Reena and act natural. Remember the fingerprints," she murmurs to herself, reassurance and fear mingling in her voice.

As she approaches the teller, her heart pounds in her chest. The teller, friendly and unsuspecting, greets her. "Good morning, Miss Reena. How can I assist you today?"

Her voice wavering, Teena responds, "I need to withdraw some cash from my account, please." She hands over Reena's identification and the withdrawal slip, her fingers brushing the documents.

The teller looks up, smiling, "Sure, Miss Reena. How much would you like to withdraw?"

Teena's mouth goes dry. "Let's say... five thousand," she replies, trying to mimic Reena's confident tone but failing to hide the fear in her eyes.

She watches the teller process the transaction, her nerves on edge, her mind racing. "I hope my fingerprints match hers," she thinks, the weight of the risk pressing down on her.

The teller hands her the cash. "Alright, here's your cash, Miss Reena. Have a great day!"

"Thank you," Teena manages to say, her voice barely above a whisper. She grabs the money, her hands still trembling, and leaves the bank.

Once outside, the cool air does little to calm her racing heart. She dials Reena's number, her fingers still shaking.

"Well? How did it go?" Reena asks over the phone, her voice full of anticipation.

"It worked, Reena! The teller didn't recognize me, and our fingerprints must be the same. Can you believe it?" Teena breathes, her voice filled with relief and astonishment.

"I knew it! We truly are exceptional twins. Even after all these years, our similarities are astonishing," Reena exclaims, laughing.

"Yes, they are. But let's not make a habit of this, okay? It was a little nerve- wracking," Teena adds, her excitement giving way to a more somber realization.

"Of course, Teena. This was just a one-time test. But now we know, don't we?" Reena's voice is warm and reassuring.

"Yes, we do. We're one of a kind," Teena replies, feeling proud, reassured, and connected to her sister.

They end the call, and Teena walks away, the pride of her accomplishment mingling with a lingering sense of fear and excitement. The connection she shares with her twin sister Reena has been tested and proven once more, yet the danger of the game they played looms large in her mind....

Reena's beachside backyard offers a picturesque view, with gentle waves caressing the shore and the sun smiling down on the world. Seated at a table overlooking the beach, Reena and Teena, the exceptional twins, enjoy casual drinks, reflecting on the day's events.

Reena, looking thoughtful and still in awe of their adventure, begins, "So, the bank didn't suspect anything? That's really something, Teena."

Teena grins, the excitement of the day still fresh in her eyes. "Not a single clue. I acted just like you, even worried about the fingerprints."

Reena leans back, her professional curiosity piqued. "That's incredible! In my professional field, I've seen cases of identical twins with similar minutiae, bifurcations, and ridge endings, but a perfect match like ours is unheard of."

Teena's eyes widen, intrigued by the technical jargon. "You make it sound so technical. But the real question is, have you ever come across identical like us?"

Reena's gaze turns reflective, her eyes fixed on the distant horizon. "Not quite like us. There may be others out there, but the world doesn't know about them. Our connection is unique."

Teena leans in, her voice teasing, "Yeah, we're going to confuse our future husbands too!"

They both burst into laughter, the sound mingling with the gentle rustle of the sea breeze. Reena adds, still chuckling, "Oh, yeah... we can exchange with both of them."

Teena, her eyes sparkling with mischief, continues, "It's going to be CRAZY!"

Chapter 3.

31

They share a toast, their glasses clinking together, and a light-hearted laugh, basking in the warm glow of their unique bond. The sun begins to set over the horizon, painting the sky with shades of orange and pink, providing a perfect backdrop to their conversation.

Max, a small and energetic dog, suddenly runs into the scene, his tail wagging. He jumps up, trying to get the twins' attention, his joyful bark breaking through their contemplation.

Teena bends down, petting Max affectionately. "Look at him, Reena. He's as excited about our day as we are!"

Reena smiles, joining her sister in petting their furry friend. "Max always knows when something special has happened."

They continue to chat, their laughter and conversation blending with the sounds of the waves and the distant call of seagulls, the connection between them emphasized by their exceptional nature.

As the day turns to evening, they linger at the table, the connection between them deepening, their shared experiences binding them together in a way few can understand. The world around them may continue to move, but for Reena and Teena, this moment is a celebration of their unique bond.

Teena lounges on the plush sofa in Reena's living room, phone in hand, chatting with her close friend Sarah. The room is filled with the familiar warmth of friendship as they both laugh and joke about various topics.

"Sarah, I swear," Teena laughs, "you could make a career out of stand-up comedy!"

Sarah replies jokingly, "Well, I've got to entertain myself somehow. Speaking of which, have you had any more visions of your 'love at first sight' man?"

Teena's voice takes on a dreamy quality as she sighs, "Oh, don't even get me started. I can't get him out of my head!"

"Should I play detective for you?" Sarah teases. "I can go on a wild manhunt!"

"Please do!" Teena exclaims, laughing again. "Just find me someone as good- looking as him!"

"Deal! But only if he has a twin for me." Sarah's voice is playful as they both laugh, enjoying a moment of shared dreams and excitement.

Teena's tone becomes more serious. "But seriously, Sarah, did you find any clue about him?"

"I'm still scanning the city with my 'dream man' radar," Sarah jokes. "No hits yet, but I'll keep you posted!"

They both laugh, and the conversation ends on a high note.

Los Angeles, an audition room filled with nervous energy. Aspiring models pace back and forth, some deep in thought, others engaging in hushed conversations. The air is thick with anticipation.

"Talent Scout!" calls out a voice. "John, you're next."

John's heart jumps. He takes a deep breath and stands, gathering his portfolio. His eyes shine with determination.

"Wish me luck, guys," he says confidently. "See you on the other side."

"Knock 'em dead, John!" a female co-aspirant says, her voice supportive.

John enters the audition room, leaving the door slightly ajar. The rest of the hopefuls strain to hear any indication of how it's going.

Inside the audition stage, the room is stark, lit only by bright studio lights. A panel of judges sits at a long table, their faces inscrutable.

"Welcome, John," says the lead judge, her voice professional. "Let's see what you've got."

John's nerves almost get the better of him, but he recalls his determination and the support of his fellow aspirants. "Thank you for this opportunity," he says confidently. "I promise I won't let you down."

He begins to walk, strike poses, and engage with the camera, letting his passion and hard work shine through.

"Interesting," the lead judge nods appreciatively. "You've certainly got a unique look."

The other judges murmur in agreement, jotting down notes.

"Thank you," John says humbly. "I've put everything into this, and I'm ready for whatever comes next."

"Very well," the lead judge says firmly. "We'll be in touch. Next!"

John exits, the door closing behind him. He re-enters the waiting room, a mixture of relief and uncertainty on his face.

"Well? How did it go?" a male co-aspirant asks eagerly.

"I'm not sure," John replies thoughtfully. "They seemed interested, but you never know."

The others nod, understanding the uncertainty of the industry.

"You did your best, and that's what matters," a female co-aspirant encourages.

They continue to exchange stories and encouragement, knowing that regardless of the outcome, they've all shared a common experience, growing, and learning together.

In the quaint and picturesque town of Carmel, where the streets are lined with beautiful buildings and vibrant gardens, sisters Teena and Reena decide to embark on a day of adventure. They explore various places, feeling the pulse of the small town, before setting their sights on a breathtaking hilltop. As they drive closer, the path leading to the hilltop reveals itself to be risky and steep. The winding road is filled with loose stones that make the climb treacherous, each turn hinting at danger.

Undeterred, they make their way up, the car navigating the rugged terrain. Reena's puppy, Max, whines with excitement from the back seat, sensing the adventure ahead. The two sisters share a glance, excitement gleaming in their eyes.

Finally, after a suspense-filled journey, they reach the top, and the scene that greets them takes their breath away. The hilltop overlooks a deep valley below, where rolling hills meet dense forests. The lush greenery paints a serene picture, and the way the sunlight dances on the leaves makes it seem as though the whole valley is alive.

Teena holds Max in her arms, and the little furball seems to have a special affinity for her. They both look out at the view, mesmerized by its grandeur.

"Hey, Max, why do you always prefer Teena over me? Aren't I your favorite owner?" Reena playfully asks, feigning hurt.

Max wiggles in Teena's arms, his tail wagging, showing no signs of wanting to leave her side.

"Seems like Max knows who his true favorite is. Don't worry; he loves you too, but he has a soft spot for me," Teena teases, a mischievous grin playing on her lips.

As they enjoy the stunning view from the hilltop, Max suddenly becomes curious about something and squirms in Teena's arms. His eyes fixated, he jumps out of her arms and dashes toward the edge of the dangerous point.

"Max, no! Come back!" Reena panics, her heart racing with fear.

Teena, however, remains calm. With careful precision, she moves to the edge and manages to catch Max just in time, saving him from any harm.

"It's alright, Max. You can't be too adventurous like me," Teena gently scolds, holding him close.

Reena, relieved and grateful, hugs Max tightly. "Thank you, Teena. I don't know what I would have done if anything happened to him."

"No need to worry. I've got my eyes on him," Teena smiles, her voice filled with reassurance.

Throughout the day, Reena receives calls on her phone, some serious and others lighthearted. Teena observes Reena's different expressions while on the phone, sometimes serious and other times beaming with a smile.

As the day comes to a close, the sisters sit together on the hilltop, basking in the beauty of the setting sun. The golden rays cast a warm glow over the landscape, illuminating their faces as they reflect on the importance of family, connection, joy, and balance. They share a moment of peaceful silence, their hearts filled with gratitude for the simple joys of life...

Reena and Teena's birthday celebration was an event that dazzled the eyes and warmed the hearts of all present. Held in a luxurious hotel with grand chandeliers and opulent décor, the room was abuzz with laughter and cheer. The two sisters, dressed identically in stunning gowns that sparkled under the soft lighting, were the stars of the evening.

Guests mingled, exchanging greetings and compliments, all the while marveling at the uncanny resemblance between Reena and Teena.

"Reena, Happy birthday! I must say, you both look stunning in your matching outfits," one guest gushed, while another queried, "Wait, are you two twins?"

"Yes, we are identical twins, and it's our special day," Reena replied, her smile as radiant as the jewels she wore.

"I can't believe how much you two look alike!" a third guest exclaimed, eyes wide with fascination.

Reena took the opportunity to introduce Teena to her office colleagues and friends, beaming with pride. "Everyone, this is my sister, Teena. She's the artistic one in the family."

Teena grinned, her eyes sparkling with excitement. "Nice to meet you all. Thank you for being here to celebrate with us."

The party was lively, filled with laughter, and even Max, the adorable puppy, happily greeted everyone with a wagging tail.

The moment to cut the cake arrived, and the boss, a man with an enthusiastic spirit, called out, "Alright, it's time to cut the cake!"

But Reena hesitated, her eyes glancing towards the entrance. "I'm sorry, but I'm waiting for an important guest. Please wait just a little longer."

The anticipation in the room grew, the air thick with curiosity. And then, like a sudden gust of wind, the unexpected happened.

John, the unannounced but awaited guest, arrived at the celebration. Tall and dashing, he entered the room with a confident stride, his eyes scanning the crowd. Spotting Teena from behind and mistaking her for Reena, he approached her with a glint of affection in his eyes.

In one swift motion, he embraced her, turning her around and planting a passionate kiss on her lips.

Teena was taken aback, her heart pounding in her chest. Her eyes widened in surprise, and for a moment, she was unable to find the right words to respond. Her mind raced her emotions a whirlpool of confusion, excitement, and disbelief.

But then, John's eyes met hers, and his face registered a look of confusion. He looked around and spotted another woman behind, so identical to the one he had just kissed. His eyes widened, and his face turned pale, realizing his mistake.

The room fell into a stunned silence, all eyes on the trio, as they tried to make sense of what had just happened. The air was charged with a mixture of shock, amusement, and curiosity.

But what no one in that room realized was that in that single, unexpected kiss, something profound had been awakened. A connection, unspoken but undeniable, had been forged between Teena and John. A connection that transcended mere physical attraction, touching something deep and elemental.

The celebration continued, but in Teena's heart, a new chapter had just begun. A chapter filled with intrigue, romance, and the promise of something extraordinary. For in that one fleeting moment, she had found the man she had been searching for, the man from the park, her love at first sight.

The evening would go on, but that single moment would remain etched in Teena's memory, a turning point that would change the course of her life forever.

The atmosphere is vibrant as the birthday celebration continues in the hotel's elegant ballroom, adorned with glittering chandeliers and tastefully decorated tables. Reena and Teena stand together as the cake is brought out. They take the knife, their bond evident in their synchronized actions. With a smile, they cut the cake together, symbolizing their unbreakable connection as twins.

As the guests cheered and clapped, Reena playfully leaned over and kissed John so emotionally, making him blush. Laughter filled the room as Reena teased, "Make a wish, John!" John chuckled and blew out the candle, the light- hearted atmosphere captivating everyone present.

The party continued in full swing, and Reena, John, and Teena found themselves at a table together. Reena introduced her sister with a warm smile. "John, this is my sister, Teena. Teena, meet John."

John looked into Teena's eyes, apologetic. "Teena, about the earlier misunderstanding... I never meant to—"

"No need to apologize, John. It happens," Teena interrupted, her eyes flickering with an unreadable emotion. Something stirred within her as she looked at John, a nagging sense of recognition.

As the night progressed, Reena and John danced gracefully to the music, their joy evident in their movements. Teena sat, observing them with a calm exterior but a whirlwind of emotions inside. Her heart ached as she watched them together, knowing that John was the one she had been longing for, but also understanding that he was now a part of Reena's life.

Teena's mind was a storm of conflicting emotions as she watched the celebration, torn between a profound connection to a stranger and loyalty to her sister. The next day, the sun glistened over the calm ocean waves as Teena swam, her strokes powerful and determined. Her heart was a storm of love, longing, and guilt, reflected in the rhythm of the waves.

She struggled with her feelings for John, whispering to herself, "How could this happen? Of all the people in the world, why him? Why now?" Her determination grew as she thought, "I can't let this affect our bond. Reena deserves happiness, and I won't stand in her way."

Eventually, she reached calmness and exited the water, her skin glistening. She called her friend Sarah, her voice breaking slightly. "Sarah, can we talk? I need someone to talk to."

Sarah "What's bothering you?"

"It's so complicated, Sarah. He's the one I've been searching for, but he's with Reena now. I don't know what to do."

"Teena, sometimes life throws us these unexpected challenges. You'll find someone who's perfect for you. Focus on being there for your sister."

With renewed determination, Teena dived back into the water, the vast ocean a symbol of her inner strength.

John and Reena later sat on the edge of the hilltop, the twinkling lights of the small town below casting a romantic glow. John shared his struggles to become a model, his voice soft and reflective. Reena's support was unwavering as she expressed her faith in him.

Their conversation turned to their relationship, and Reena's eyes sparkled with determination as she told John, "I want to be your wife."

John was deeply touched, and they exchanged loving words, promising to face anything together. They sealed their promise with a deep, loving kiss, their silhouettes lingering against the distant lights.

Their love was profound, transcending mere words and gestures. A love nurtured by time, shared dreams, and struggles; a bond grown stronger with each passing day. Their warmth, tenderness, and unspoken understanding created an expression of love that needed no words. It was a love that promised to endure, grow, and inspire, for the rest of their lives.

Teena stood in the living room, her heart heavy with conflicting emotions. She knew she had to face reality and make a decision. Her sister, Reena, bounced into the room, eyes sparkling with excitement.

"Teena, you won't believe it! John and I have decided to get married next month," Reena exclaimed.

Teena forced a smile, trying to hide her own feelings of heartache. She took a deep breath before responding. "Wow, Reena, that's amazing news! I'm so happy for both of you."

"Thank you, sis. Your love and support mean the world to me," Reena said, hugging Teena tightly. As Reena's arms encircled her, Teena's heart ached, knowing that the man she loved would now be forever out of her reach.

She took another deep breath and gathered the courage to speak. "Reena, I've to go back to my place for a while. There are some things I need to sort out."

"Go back? But, Teena, the wedding is not even a month away. Can't you stay a little longer?" Reena asked, her voice tinged with surprise.

Teena hesitated, not wanting to hurt her sister, but she knew she couldn't stay and watch the man she loved marry someone else. "I know, Reena, and I promise I'll be back before the wedding. There's just something I need to take care of."

Reena looked disappointed, not fully convinced by Teena's explanation. "But the time is so short, Teena. I wanted you to be here with me through all the wedding preparations."

"I'll make it work, Reena. Trust me. And besides, you have a lot on your plate for the wedding. You should focus on that," Teena reassured her sister.

Reena looked torn, wanting her sister to stay but also understanding that Teena had her reasons. "Alright but promise me you'll be back soon. I don't want you to miss any of the wedding festivities."

"I promise, Reena. I'll be back in time for all the celebrations," Teena said sincerely.

"Thank you, Teena. You're the best sister anyone could ask for. Now, come on, we have a lot to discuss before you leave. Let's not talk about the wedding now. We can plan everything once you're back," Reena smiled, embracing her sister.

They stood together, Reena's excitement for her upcoming marriage tinged with concern for her sister, and Teena's support shadowed by her unspoken love for John. Though the wedding plans remained unspoken for now, the connection between the sisters was strong, their bond unbreakable even in the face of unspoken truths.

The room was abuzz with laughter and chatter as John's cousins and other family members gathered in the cozy living room of his childhood home in Carmel. Framed pictures of their shared memories adorned the walls, and the soft glow of the lamps added to the celebratory mood. They were toasting John's upcoming wedding with Reena, a topic that brought smiles to everyone's faces.

"So, John, where do you plan to stay after the marriage?" his cousin sister asked, her eyes sparkling with genuine curiosity. She had seen John grow up, and his wedding was a significant moment for their close-knit family.

John paused, taking a thoughtful sip of his drink. The weight of the decision lingered in his mind, but he knew his path. "For now, I'll be staying at Reena's house. My modeling career has me moving around a lot, so I haven't thought about a permanent place yet."

His cousin brother playfully nudged him, a teasing grin spreading across his face. "Ah, the life of a nomadic model! But seriously, John, have you considered settling down in one place eventually?" He knew John's ambitious nature well and was both challenging and encouraging to him.

John chuckled, the question not catching him off guard. "Of course, I have. But right now, my focus is on building my career and making the most of the opportunities that come my way."

His cousin sister's eyes softened, her support for John palpable. "That makes sense. You should follow your dreams and see where they take you."

John's heart swelled with gratitude. "Thanks. It means a lot to have all of you behind me," he said, feeling the sincere love and understanding that only family could offer.

His aunt, who had been quietly watching, finally spoke, her voice a gentle reminder of wisdom and age. "We know Reena, she is a good girl. You will be happy in her true love." Her words were a stamp of approval, reassuring John in his choice.

As the evening wore on, the conversation ebbed and flowed, touching on old memories and future hopes. John found comfort in the familial warmth and the knowledge that they were there for him during this special time in his life. They understood his unconventional decision to stay at Reena's house and respected his commitment to his dreams.

The laughter continued, the toasts were raised, and John felt more connected to his roots than ever before, knowing that his family's love and blessings were with him as he embarked on this new journey with Reena.

Chapter 4.

48

Reena's heart pounded with a mixture of nervous excitement as she stood before her office colleagues in the breakroom. A fresh pot of coffee brewed in the background, and the aroma filled the room, but the familiar scent did nothing to ease her butterflies. Today, she was going to share something special, something close to her heart, and she could hardly contain her joy.

With a beaming smile, she clasped her hands together and began, "I have an announcement to make, everyone. I'm getting married!"

The room erupted with cheers and applause, the excitement contagious as it spread from one person to another. Friendly faces smiled back at her, eyes twinkling with genuine happiness for their colleague and friend.

"Oh, that's wonderful news, Reena! Congratulations!" one of her colleagues exclaimed, excitement ringing in her voice.

A playful response followed from another colleague, "Finally! We've been waiting for this day."

Reena's laughter mingled with the celebratory sounds, her cheeks flushed with joy. "I know, I know. It took a while, but I couldn't be happier."

A curious voice piped up, "Tell us more about the lucky guy. Is he from here?"

Blushing, Reena filled them in on the details. "His name is John, you all saw him at my birthday party. He's an aspirant model, and we met a few years ago in this town."

An intrigued colleague raised an eyebrow, admiration in her eyes. "A model? Wow, he must be quite the catch!"

Pride swelled within Reena as she nodded, "He definitely is. But more than that, he's kind, supportive, and understands my crazy schedule."

Teasing laughter followed as another colleague chimed in, "Well, we can't wait to meet him! When's the big day?"

Reena's smile widened, her eyes gleaming with anticipation. "We're still finalizing the details, but it will be in about a month. I'll keep you all posted."

As the gathering continued, Reena found herself immersed in the warmth of her colleagues' support and well-wishes. Questions flowed, and she answered each with an open heart, sharing more details about the wedding plans.

They were more than just coworkers; they were friends who had become part of her daily life. They shared lunches, late nights, and many cups of coffee.

Now, they were sharing one of the most significant moments in her life, and Reena couldn't have wished for a better group to celebrate with.

The excitement in the room lingered long after the announcements, an undercurrent of joy that would carry Reena through the busy weeks ahead. Her colleagues were thrilled for her, eager to be part of the special day, and their happiness only added to Reena's own.

As she returned to her desk, Reena felt a contentment settle within her. Everything was falling into place, and she knew that with her friends by her side, the journey to her wedding day would be as beautiful as the life she was building with John.

Teena's heart was light as she walked briskly on the footpath, her arms laden with grocery bags filled with fresh food items for Reena's fridge. She was set to fly to New York that evening, and the excitement of her upcoming journey mingled with a touch of anxiety. Her mind was too occupied with pleasant thoughts to worry much.

Her step had a bounce to it, her smile wide, but as she rounded a corner, her world came crashing down. A teenage boy, reckless on his bicycle, came speeding around the same bend, colliding with Teena in a blur of motion.

"Oh no!" Teena cried out, startled.

The sudden impact caused her to stumble and fall, the grocery bags scattering, their contents spilling onto the ground. Pain shot through her ankle like a hot knife, and she grimaced in agony, her hand clutching at the injured spot.

"Ouch! My ankle," she moaned, tears welling in her eyes.

The boy stopped his bicycle, his face pale, his eyes wide with worry. "I'm so sorry! I didn't see you coming."

Teena, biting her lip to hold back a cry of pain, attempted to stand. "It's okay, just be more careful next time."

But as she tried to put weight on her ankle, reality set in. It wasn't okay. She couldn't stand. She sat back down, wincing, her voice tinged with concern. "Actually, I might need some help."

Later, at the hospital, Teena's ankle was bandaged and securely wrapped after an X-ray confirmed a fracture. Reena stood by her side, her face etched with worry, her hands wringing together.

"You've got a minor fracture, nothing too serious," the doctor informed Teena. "But you'll need to keep weight off that ankle and take it easy for at least two weeks."

Teena nodded, a forced smile on her face. "Got it. Thank you, Doctor."

Reena helped her sister into a wheelchair, her touch gentle, her voice filled with concern. "Take it easy, okay? We'll take care of everything."

As Reena wheeled Teena out into the hospital lobby, John, who had been waiting anxiously, approached, his brow furrowed with worry. "Is everything alright?"

"Teena has a fracture. She needs rest for a couple of weeks," Reena explained, her voice catching.

John's face fell, concern etched in his features. "I'm so sorry to hear that."

Teena managed a weak smile, her eyes shining with unshed tears. "It's okay. I'll be fine."

John offered his support, helping Teena into the back seat of the car with gentle hands. "Let me help you get comfortable."

Teena settled in, gratitude in her eyes, her body aching but her spirit unbroken. "No, I'm going. I'll rest there."

Her determination was clear, but so was her discomfort. Reena hugged her sister gently before closing the car door, her eyes filled with concern. "Just promise me you won't push yourself too hard."

As the car drove away, Teena watched her sister and John through the window, a mixture of emotions playing across her face. The excitement of the journey to New York was now overshadowed by pain and worry, but her resolve was unshaken. She would go on, even if it meant bearing the weight of her injury, for the adventure ahead was too precious to miss.

Reena's home was abuzz with the joyful chaos of wedding preparations. Teena, despite the fracture in her ankle, was determined to participate and contribute to her sister's happiness.

In the kitchen, Reena was preparing a meal, taking special care to make Teena's favorite dishes. Teena was seated at the dining table, her injured ankle propped up, her eyes shining with a mix of excitement and frustration.

"Here you go," Reena said, feeding Teena with a spoon. Her voice was gentle, tinged with concern for her sister's injury. "Eat up, and you'll feel better."

Teena smiled weakly, trying to savor the food but unable to shake the nagging pain in her ankle. She appreciated Reena's care but couldn't help feeling like a burden. "I wish I could do more to help," she said, her voice cracking.

"You're doing more than enough," Reena reassured her, her hand briefly touching Teena's. "Your presence here means everything to me."

The days passed in a whirlwind of activity. Reena and John, handling both office work and wedding arrangements, were a picture of determination and excitement. John's video calls with modeling agencies were punctuated by laughter and shared glances with Reena, as they planned their future together.

Teena, despite her struggles with the injury, remained resolute. She wanted to be part of the joyous preparations, even if it meant pushing through the pain. Her bedroom became her heaven, a place to rest and reflect.

A call from her friend Sarah provided a welcome distraction. "In a few hours before catching the flight, this fracture happened. I am in pain, as you know. The fracture added to it... it's my fate," Teena confided, her voice trembling.

"Oh, come on, Teena! Don't let a little fracture ruin your spirit. You've got this! Remember, you're my strong and fearless friend," Sarah encouraged, her voice full of warmth and affection.

Teena smiled, her spirits lifted by Sarah's words. "You're right, Sarah. Thanks for cheering me up. I needed that."

They spent the rest of the call sharing jokes and laughter, a bright spot in Teena's day that helped her momentarily forget her worries.

Meanwhile, the wedding preparations continued unabated. John and Reena were a seamless team, their love and understanding deepening as they worked together. The living room was filled with fabric swatches, flower arrangements, and guest lists, but the overwhelming feeling was one of joy and anticipation.

In their hearts, they all knew that the wedding would be a celebration not just of love, but of family, resilience, and the power of human connection.

Reena's arrival at home is marked by genuine warmth as she and her sister Teena embrace each other tightly. The joyful reunion, filled with love and understanding, even has their puppy joining in, though not without some hesitation. At first, the little canine seems unsure, sensing a shift in emotions, but then, perhaps driven by curiosity or recognizing the bond between the sisters, it draws near, circling around them as it sniffs and examines them with innocent eyes.

Reena's attention shifts to Teena's ankle, concern creasing her brow. Her gentle fingers touch the area, examining it with care. "How's your ankle feeling now? Can you walk without much pain?" she asks, her voice filled with compassion.

"It's better, sis. Still a little sore, but I can manage," Teena replies, her smile genuine but guarded.

Relief washes over Reena's face, and she can't help but hug her sister again. "I'm so glad to hear that," she says, her voice filled with gratitude.

Together, they move to the kitchen, a place filled with familiar scents and memories. The clatter of utensils, the sizzle of oil, and their laughter weave together a scene of domestic harmony as they prepare a meal. They chatted excitedly about the wedding, Reena's voice bubbling with anticipation, "The wedding day is not too far now. I can't wait to marry John."

Teena's response is supportive but restrained, "I know. It's going to be a beautiful day," she says, her smile forced, not quite reaching her eyes. The sisters discuss the arrangements, but all the while, Teena's mind is awhirl with conflicting emotions.

Later, in the quiet sanctity of the bedroom, Reena drifts off to peaceful slumber, her face relaxed and content. But Teena lies awake, her mind in turmoil. She gazes at her sister, her eyes filled with love, guilt, and confusion. The complexity of her feelings for John and the looming wedding casts a shadow over her heart.

The room is filled with the gentle rustle of sheets and the distant sounds of the night. Teena's eyes well up with tears, and the weight of her emotions becomes almost tangible in the silence. A single tear escapes, trailing down her cheek, and she turns away, burying her face in her pillow.

As the night deepens, the room settles into a pensive silence, the only sound being Teena's soft, troubled breaths. Her mind continues to wrestle with her feelings, leaving her adrift in a sea of uncertainty and longing.

Reena's living room is alive with the pulsating rhythm of celebration. Delicate flowers and twinkling lights festoon the room, casting a soft glow on the faces of friends and family. Laughter and clinking glasses fill the air, and the atmosphere is abuzz with joy and excitement.

Teena and Reena stand at the heart of it all, surrounded by well-wishers. A guest lifts his glass, eyes sparkling with genuine warmth, "Here's to the beautiful bride-to-be, Reena, and her charming groom, John. May their love shine forever!" A chorus of cheers follows, and everyone drinks to the toast. The sound of clinking glasses mingles with laughter, creating a melody of happiness.

Teena turns to her sister, a smile lighting her face, but in her eyes, a shadow of something unspoken lurks. "I couldn't be happier for you, Reena. You two make a perfect couple," she says, her voice filled with affection yet tinged with melancholy.

Reena, radiant in her blushing joy, leans in and whispers, "Thanks, Teena. You've been my rock throughout all this. I'm so grateful to have you as my sister." They embrace, but as they pull away, Teena's eyes reveal a hidden pain. The room continues to hum with celebration, but an undercurrent of tension begins to emerge.

Chapter 5.

57

The atmosphere changes abruptly and suddenly plunged into the cold, unsettling silence of Mr. Anderson's house at night. The once familiar surroundings now seem ominous, filled with shadows and uncertainty.

Mr. Anderson's face, pale and drawn, is etched with worry as he rushes through the door. The silence greets him like a physical blow. "Honey? Are you here?" he calls, his voice trembling with fear. The absence of a response sends a chill down his spine.

Stepping outside, a nightmarish sight awaits him: his wife, Martha, lying on the ground, her face contorted in pain, body bruised and battered. Panic seizes him as he falls to his knees beside her, his hands shaking as they reach out to touch her.

"What happened? Who did this to you?" he chokes out, his voice cracking with desperation and terror.

Martha's eyes, filled with pain and fear, meet his. She whispers, her voice barely audible, "They warned me, David. They said to make you stop the investigation, or else..."

Rage ignites within Mr. Anderson, burning away the fear. His voice becomes steely as he declares, "I won't be silenced, not by them or anyone else. We've come too far to back down now."

As he dials for an ambulance, his mind races, consumed by fear for his wife and a growing thirst for justice. The distant wail of sirens grows nearer, but in the stillness of the night, the sense of danger lingers, tangible and menacing.

In the hospital's waiting area, under the harsh glare of fluorescent lights, a group of Mr. Anderson's staff and close friends have gathered. Among them, Reena, her face etched with concern, appears visibly shaken. The sterile scent of antiseptic fills the air as everyone anxiously awaits news.

A senior employee, his voice strained with worry, speaks on the phone. "Yes, it's a difficult situation, but you know Mr. Anderson. He's never been one to back down from the truth. He's always stood up for what's right, no matter the risks."

The others in the room nod, their faces filled with both fear and acknowledgment of Mr. Anderson's unwavering commitment to journalism and truth.

In the adjacent hospital room, Mrs. Anderson, known as Martha, lies in the hospital bed, her eyes wide with fear, still shaken from the incident. The police, their expressions somber and focused, arrive to take her statement.

The police officer, his voice both kind and firm, asks, "Mrs. Anderson, we need to understand what happened. Can you tell us anything about the attackers?"

Martha's voice trembles as she responds, "I didn't see their faces clearly. They warned me to make David stop his investigation into the scandal, or they would hurt us again."

The officer assures her, his voice carrying a sense of urgency, "We'll do everything we can to catch those responsible. But we need your help with any information you can provide. This is a priority case."

Martha provides what little information she has, her determination matching that of the police officers, who take diligent notes.

Back in the waiting area, the staff and friends offer their support, standing together in solidarity. Reena holds back tears, her heart heavy with worry for her boss and his family. Her voice filled with conviction, she says to a friend, "We need to find those responsible and make sure they face justice. We owe it to Mr. Anderson."

Her friend nods fiercely, responding, "Don't worry, Reena. We won't rest until we get to the bottom of this. We'll support Mr. Anderson all the way."

A sense of unity binds the group, their voices tinged with urgency, determined to stand by Mr. Anderson and support him in any way possible. The underlying tension in the room hints at the danger and complexity of the investigation, leaving a palpable sense of unease that lingers long after their words have been spoken.

Teena was in the kitchen, lost in her world, smiling at her own absent- mindedness. The forgotten salt and the TV remote had become the amusing topic of conversation with her friend Sarah. Laughter and shared understanding danced in their voices.

In the living room, Reena's face was drawn tight with worry. The recent incidents, upcoming wedding, and professional threats were a heavy burden. Her phone conversation with a colleague added to the stress, leaving her feeling overwhelmed.

At the hospital, Mr. Anderson's room was filled with warmth and grace. Visitors came and went, and Reena's appearance was marked by her visible tension.

Mr. Anderson's soft words to her were meant to calm her worries about the situation.

"Don't worry, Reena. Focus on your happiness. Your marriage is a joyous occasion, and nothing should overshadow that," he told her, his eyes gentle and understanding.

Later, in the hospital parking lot, he approached her again, sensing her preoccupation. His voice was soft, reassuring as he encouraged her to focus on the love and joy of her upcoming wedding.

"Reena, my dear, I know you have a lot on your plate right now, but don't let anything overshadow the joy of this special time. The wedding is a celebration of love, and I want to see you marry with a smile on your face," he said, his eyes warm with genuine concern.

Reena's eyes filled with gratitude. "Thank you, Mr. Anderson. It's just been overwhelming lately, and I don't know if I'm managing everything well."

He patted her hand encouragingly, his voice filled with fatherly affection. "Life is full of ups and downs, but love and family are what truly matter. Focus on your happiness with John. You've got all our support. We believe in you, Reena."

Driving away, Reena felt a new sense of clarity and determination. Mr. Anderson's words had given her strength, and she was now more than ever focused on the love she shared with John. The road ahead was still complex, but she knew they would navigate it together. Her heart swelled with anticipation and love, the horizon clear and inviting.

The church was beautifully adorned with a sea of flowers, their sweet fragrance mingling with the soft notes of the organ. Cascades of soft, satin ribbons hung elegantly from the pews, catching the sunlight that filtered through the stained glass windows, creating a spectacle of love and joy.

Reena was radiant in her wedding gown, every step she took shimmering with excitement. Her smile was wide, her eyes sparkling, but it was her happiness that truly shone. She was marrying the man she loved, and nothing else mattered.

Teena, though happy for her beloved sister, carried a hint of pain as she watched her first love marry someone else. Her eyes were filled with mixed emotions, a smile on her lips, but a small, hidden ache in her heart.

As the wedding ceremony proceeded, all their friends, family, and colleagues gathered to witness the union. John's cousins, Anderson with Martha, and Reena's office staff were all in attendance, including Puppy, who added a touch of charm to the occasion.

The ceremony was filled with moments that touched the hearts of everyone present. As the priest pronounced them husband and wife, John and Reena faced each other, eyes locked, hands trembling with emotion. With a smile that spoke of infinite love, John took Reena's hand and delicately slid the ring onto her finger. The cool metal glinted in the soft light, a symbol of their eternal commitment.

Reena, her eyes filled with tears of joy, reciprocated the gesture, placing John's ring on her finger. Their fingers lingered for a moment, the rings a tangible connection between them, a promise of a life filled with love.

Then they kissed, a loving kiss that sealed their commitment to each other. It was a moment that seemed to stop time, a kiss that promised a lifetime of love and trust.

After the ceremony, Teena approached John with courage in her step and playfulness in her eyes. She lightly touched his cheek and whispered, "Marry me too." John just laughed, and Teena smiled back, trying to mask her true feelings.

She knew that John was now off-limits for her, but a small part of her couldn't help but hold on to the memory of their brief connection. As the night came to a close, Teena bid farewell to the newlyweds, their friends, and the guests.

She watched as John and Reena drove off into their new life together, her heart heavy with bittersweet emotions. Her eyes followed the car until it disappeared into the horizon, and she was left standing there, a smile on her face, but a longing in her heart, knowing that a chapter of her life had closed, but grateful for the love and joy she had witnessed.

Teena sat at her desk, a pen in hand, her thoughts spilling onto the paper with the ink. She was writing a heartfelt letter to Reena, wishing her a lifetime of love and happiness in her married life. Alongside the letter, she included a small, delicate piece of art—a symbolic symbol of their bond and love for each other. Her hand gracefully penned the lines that captured the essence of their sisterly connection:

"In hearts entwined, forever bound, A love like ours knows no confine,

Though paths diverge, we'll still be near, Sisters in soul, forever dear."

The words resonated with her emotions, a parting gift filled with love and hope.

The next day was filled with bittersweet moments as she handed over Puppy to a dog caretaker. Her eyes welled up as she bid farewell to her furry companion, knowing that this separation was for the best as she embarked on a new journey to New York.

Meanwhile, in a hotel room, John and Reena lost themselves in each other's embrace, their connection deepening in a passionate expression of love.

Reena's face radiated sheer joy and contentment as they shared a moment of profound intimacy.

Teena's journey continued as she and Sarah drove back to her apartment from the airport. Teena's heart was heavy, filled with the complex emotions of love, loss, excitement, and anticipation. She opened up to Sarah, her voice tinged with both joy and sadness as she described the beauty of the marriage bond she had witnessed at Reena's wedding.

"Sarah, you should have seen Reena today," Teena said, a smile playing on her lips. "She looked so beautiful and happy. Her eyes were shining with love and joy. It was such a magical moment."

Sarah grinned back at her. "I can only imagine. Reena has found her perfect match in John, hasn't she?"

Teena nodded, her eyes distant. "Yes, she has. And I couldn't be happier for her. Love is a beautiful thing, isn't it? Seeing them together, I felt the power of their connection, the strength of their love."

They talked more, Teena expressing her feelings, acknowledging the pain of letting go of her first love, but also the excitement of starting afresh in New York. Her voice quivered with a mix of resolve and nostalgia.

"I will be okay," she said, pausing to smile at Sarah. "It's a bit hard to let go, but I know this is the right path for both of us. New York holds so many opportunities, and I'm ready to embrace them."

And they talked on, Sarah encouraging her, supporting her, reassuring her that distance would not break the bond she shared with Reena. They spoke of new adventures, of embracing life with an open heart.

Teena's eyes shone with determination. "I will, Sarah. Thank you for being here for me, always."

As the car continued on its journey, Teena's heart was filled with a strange mixture of emotions. There was a sense of loss, a longing for what was left behind, but also excitement for what lay ahead. She knew that she was on the right path, that new adventures awaited her, and that she had the strength and support to embrace them fully. Her heart was open, her mind focused, and her soul ready for the journey that awaited her in New York.

The office was alive with the rhythmic tap of keyboards and the low murmur of voices. Employees, absorbed in their tasks, shuffled papers, clicked mouses, and exchanged brief, purposeful conversations. At the heart of this industrious environment sat Mr. Anderson, a seasoned and courageous media owner. His face was lined with wisdom, his eyes reflecting a determined spirit. He was a man who had seen much, and achieved much, yet remained grounded and committed to his values.

Suddenly, his phone rang, breaking the rhythmic routine of the room. Glancing at the caller ID, Mr. Anderson's brows furrowed, recognizing it as an unknown number. Curiosity piqued, he picked up the call, his tone friendly yet cautious.

"Hello, who am I speaking with?" he inquired.

The voice on the other end carried a smug quality, a smirk evident in its tone. "You know, Mr. Anderson, it's interesting how people have their weaknesses.

Some crave money, some power, some fame, but you... you're all about your family."

Mr. Anderson's face remained calm, his expression revealing nothing. There was a measured quality to his voice as he replied, "Well, you seem to know a lot about me."

The unknown caller continued, taunting and probing, laying bare Mr. Anderson's career, his hesitation, and his values. Yet, Mr. Anderson's responses were firm and composed, his love for his family a point of pride, not vulnerability.

"You're playing a dangerous game, Mr. Anderson," the caller warned menacingly. "If you don't comply, we'll make sure you and your family suffer."

The threat hung in the air, but Mr. Anderson's resolve did not waver. "Threats won't sway me. Just wait and watch. There's more to this story than you know."

The exchange continued, the tension mounting, and the caller's aggression met with Mr. Anderson's steadfast determination. When the call abruptly ended, Mr. Anderson leaned back in his chair, his mind a whirl of thoughts, yet his eyes still holding that glint of determination.

Time passed, and later in the office, Mr. Anderson gathered his senior employees, sharing the incident with them. The room was heavy with the gravity of the situation, faces etched with concern. But as Mr. Anderson spoke, his voice steady, his words imbued with conviction, a sense of reassurance settled over the team.

"My friends, we're embarking on a journey that comes with risks," he said, his eyes meeting each of theirs. "But remember, we stand for truth and justice. No matter the challenges, we'll face them together."

The team nodded in agreement, the bonds of trust and respect deepened by their leader's resilience. They were united, not only by their common goal but by the shared belief in their ability to overcome any obstacle. The room, once filled with uncertainty, now resonated with a renewed sense of purpose and courage, ready to face the storm ahead.

Teena's apartment was a sanctuary, filled with the soft glow of creativity. Sketches and paintings adorned the walls, evidence of a soul constantly reaching out for expression. Among them lay the unfinished outline of John's painting, a painful remnant of a love once cherished, now lost.

Standing by her desk, Teena's hands trembled as they held the outline, her heart warring with her mind. To destroy it would be to sever the last thread that connected her to John, yet she found herself paralyzed, unable to complete the act. With a sigh, she tucked the outline into a hidden drawer, burying it along with the memories it invoked.

"Maybe it's time to let go of the past and embrace a new beginning," she whispered to herself, the words a balm to her aching heart.

Renewed resolve fueled her movements as she picked up her brushes and colors, pouring herself into her art. The canvas became a window to her soul, each stroke a testament to her pain, her healing, and her hope. Hours passed, and the painting came to life, a powerful symbol of love lost and a strength regained.

The next day found her stepping into the pristine halls of the art gallery agency, her finished painting cradled in her arms. The Lady Boss, a figure both admired and feared, awaited her. Her presence dominated the room, her eyes sharp, her demeanor unapologetically arrogant.

"So, you're here to show me your work. Let's see what you've got," she said, her voice dripping with condescension.

Teena's excitement wavered, replaced by nerves as she presented her painting. She spoke of pain, of healing, of a soul laid bare, but the Lady Boss's eyes saw none of it.

"Hmph, pain and healing? I've seen it all before. What makes yours any different?" she snapped, dismissing Teena's work with a glance.

The words struck Teena like a physical blow, her passion met with cold indifference. The Lady Boss's critique was ruthless, her judgment final. Teena's art, her very essence, was reduced to "amateurish scribbles."

Tears threatened, but Teena's defiance rose, her voice strong as she defended her truth, her expression. The Lady Boss's smirk was a cruel punctuation to a humiliating encounter, and Teena left, her painting and her dreams momentarily shattered.

Back in the familiarity of her apartment, the tears came freely. The walls, once a gallery of inspiration, now seemed to mock her failure. She clutched her painting, sobbing, the weight of rejection a heavy burden on her shoulders.

"Why can't they see the beauty in my art? Why do they dismiss it so easily?" she cried into the silence.

But in the depths of her despair, a spark of determination flickered. Teena's art was her soul, her voice, and no one could take that away from her. Wiping her tears, she whispered a promise to herself, a vow to keep creating, to keep believing, no matter what they said.

Her apartment, once a place of defeat, transformed into a beacon of hope, filled with the warmth of her resolve. Teena's journey as an artist was far from over; it had only just begun...

The air in the office was thick with anticipation and uncertainty. Reena and her colleagues gathered, their faces reflecting concern as they whispered about Anderson's unexpected delay in exposing the collected scandal. The room was filled with the usual buzz of phones and clattering keyboards, but the underlying tension was palpable.

"Have you noticed that Anderson seems hesitant to proceed?" Colleague 1 asked, his voice barely above a whisper.

"Yeah, something's holding him back. We need to find out why," Colleague 2 responded, his eyes darting toward Anderson's empty cabin.

All eyes turned to Reena, her closeness to Anderson making her the natural choice to approach him. She hesitated, her respect for Anderson's privacy warring with the importance of their cause. But the earnest faces of her colleagues and the weight of their shared responsibility spurred her into action.

Later, Anderson's arrival changed the atmosphere in the office. His calm demeanor and casual greeting belied the gravity of the situation, yet his eyes held a hint of determination as he headed toward his cabin. Reena followed, her heart pounding as she knocked on the door.

"Sure, Reena. What's on your mind?" Anderson's voice was warm, inviting, yet Reena could sense the underlying seriousness.

She gathered her courage, her voice steady as she posed the question that had been gnawing at them all. Anderson's response was measured, his words carefully chosen, revealing the complex nature of their mission.

"Reena, there's a lot at stake here. I need some more time to ensure everyone's safety," he said, his eyes meeting hers with unspoken understanding.

Reena nodded, her trust in Anderson's judgment absolute. The room, filled with the usual trappings of power and authority, seemed to fade into the background as they shared a moment of solidarity.

Chapter 6.

Later that night, the mood shifted entirely as Reena arrived home to find John, her face lighting up at his presence. Their home was a haven, filled with warmth and love, and John's good news brought a new spark of excitement.

"Guess what, love? I got a deal with that watch company! The shoot will happen in a month," he announced, his arms enveloping her in a hug.

Reena's joy was infectious, her belief in John's talent was validated by this success. They shared a passionate kiss, their happiness bubbling over, leading to a deeper connection, excitement leads to deeper sex. John strokes slowly and fastens peaks in-depth, Reena widens her legs for more and more... The surroundings were forgotten as they lost themselves in each other, celebrating not just the contract but their shared life and love.

In these moments, they were not colleagues or professionals; they were lovers, partners, and each other's greatest supporters. Their home, filled with personal touches and memories, became the perfect backdrop for their joy and intimacy, a testament to their bond and a reminder of what truly mattered.

In the heart of New York, amidst the city's constant movement, a pub pulsates with life. The thumping beat of the music reverberates through the floor, walls, and even the people, creating a unified rhythm of excitement. Among the revelers on the dance floor, Teena and Sarah move with an exhilarating energy, their bodies losing themselves to the music, each beat taking them farther from the worries of their daily lives.

Teena's eyes are alive, her face flushed, as she dances with wild abandon. Every twist and turn seem to be a declaration of freedom from the chains that have been binding her spirit. Sarah watches her friend, a mixture of amazement and curiosity playing in her eyes.

They've known each other for years, yet tonight something in Teena has awakened.

As the song fades, the two friends find themselves outside the pub, sitting on a bench, catching their breath, the noise of the city mingling with their laughter. Sarah's eyes widen as she looks at Teena, her surprise not hidden.

"Teena, what's happening?" Sarah's voice is tinged with both excitement and concern. "I've never seen you dance or even drink like this. What's got into you?"

A smile crosses Teena's face, genuine but tinged with sadness, her eyes reflecting a deeper pain. "Diversion, Sarah. I needed a diversion. Ever since my painting was rejected, the insult has haunted me. But I don't want to burden Reena with this, not now that she's newly married. I don't want to spoil her joy."

Sarah's eyes soften as she listens, the noise of the city fading into the background. She reaches out and takes Teena's hand, her touch a silent promise. "Teena, we all need an escape sometimes. But don't forget, you're not alone. I'm your best friend, and we share everything. I'll be here through thick and thin."

Teena's eyes glisten as she nods, visibly touched by Sarah's unwavering support. Her voice trembles slightly as she replies, "Thank you, Sarah. It's just... some things are hard to shake off. But I'll try to move forward. For now, let's enjoy the night."

With that resolve, the two friends rise, their arms around each other, the night sky above them a witness to their unbreakable bond. They head back into the pub, the music welcoming them once more, their laughter echoing through the night. The neon lights of the city seem to sparkle a little brighter, reflecting the warmth of their friendship, a balm for Teena's aching heart.

The dark and secretive city streets whisper tales of intrigue and suspense at night. Unknown individuals tail Anderson, Reena, and other staff members, their sinister silhouettes blending with the shadows. They watch with narrow, piercing eyes, communicating in hushed whispers over encrypted phones. There's a palpable sense of looming danger, a plot unfolding, the tension building in the silence.

Up above the sprawling cityscape, on Sarah's skyscraper terrace, the scene shifts to the day. Sarah, a smart, independent, and vivacious woman, shares her latest dating adventure with Teena, her eyes twinkling with mischief. "Oh, Teena, if you could have seen him last night! He looked like a peacock in human clothes! But hey, at least he tried," she laughs heartily.

Teena smirks playfully. "Well, you sure know how to pick 'em, Sarah. Keeps life interesting, doesn't it?"

Sarah grins, carefree. "That's the idea! Why settle for ordinary when you can have extraordinary?"

In Teena's cluttered apartment, a maze of failed creations, canvases with half- realized dreams, and sketches that miss the mark tell a different story. Her eyes, once bright with creativity, are now clouded with frustration, reflecting the trapped artist within. Teena, phone in hand, pours her soul out to Sarah, her voice cracking with frustration. "It's all wrong, Sarah. My hands won't listen to my heart anymore. These paintings... they're soulless."

Sarah's voice is soothing and supportive. "Teena, this is just a phase. Remember who you are, and what you're capable of. You'll get through this."

Teena sighs, defeated. "I hope so. It's painful to see my passion reduced to mediocrity."

As the sun sets and the city lights come to life, the friends find refuge either on the skyscraper terrace or within the cozy confines of Teena's apartment.

They drown their sorrows in the liquid amber of wine, laughing, crying, and toasting to life's chaos. The friends cling to each other, their laughter a facade, their smiles hiding the unspoken burdens they carry. They toast to survival, understanding that they're each other's lifeline.

"Cheers to surviving another wild day in this mad, mad world!" Teena raises her glass, half-joking.

Sarah clinks her glass, sincerely. "Cheers, Teena ! To us, and to whatever tomorrow brings!"

Reena's office is bathed in soft daylight, providing a quiet and contemplative setting. She sits alone, a dreamy expression on her face, surrounded by the familiar clutter of her desk. Her eyes fixate on her wedding ring, a symbol of her new journey, delicately tracing it with her fingers. A smile plays on her lips, but a hint of loneliness lingers in her eyes. With a thoughtful sigh, she reaches for her phone, longing to connect with her sister.

In Teena's apartment, a once-inspiring sanctuary now dulled by her artistic struggles, the phone rings. Teena's face lights up when she sees Reena's name.

"Hey, sis! Your voice is like a ray of sunshine. I missed you!" she exclaims warmly.

"I've missed you too, Teena. You're always in my thoughts. How are you holding up with your art?" Reena asks, her words an embrace.

"Oh, Reena, I feel like I'm painting shadows instead of light. My hands tremble with uncertainty," Teena confesses, a hint of sadness in her voice.

"Teena, you've painted with your soul before; you will again. Believe in yourself, as I believe in you," Reena responds, supportive and firm.

"I needed that, Reena. You always know what to say. Tell me, how's life treating you and John?" Teena inquires, grateful and teary-eyed.

"Life's a beautiful painting, Teena. John's love colors every moment. I wish you could feel what I feel," Reena replies, smiling, her heart full.

"I see it, Reena, even through the phone. You're glowing. You deserve every beautiful brushstroke," Teena says, joyful, sharing her sister's happiness.

"So do you, Teena. Your canvas awaits your brilliance. Your love story is yet to be painted," Reena assures her, her voice filled with emotion and sincerity.

"Thank you, Reena. Your faith lights my way," Teena responds, touched.

The sisters continue their conversation, painting a portrait of trust, support, and enduring love. Their words weave their dreams, fears, and hopes into the unbreakable thread that binds them, a delicate dance of empathy and encouragement. Together, they create a tapestry of connection that transcends distance, a bond painted in the colors of sisterhood.

Chapter 7.

Inside a sprawling film studio in Los Angeles, the ad shoot is in full swing. Crew members scramble across the floor, adjusting lights and setting up cameras. John's portion of the shoot takes place in a meticulously crafted living room setting. He stands aside during a break, his eyes fixed keenly on his wedding ring.

Mia, a young, beautiful co-artist, notices his gaze and smiles, her eyes gleaming with curiosity. "Who is that lucky lady?" she asks.

John's voice is soft, almost a whisper, as he answers, "That's my wife, Reena."

His words seem to hang in the air, and a connection, clear but brief, passes between them. The shoot continues around them, a whirlwind of creativity and commerce.

Meanwhile, thousands of miles away in New York, Sarah's terrace is a tranquil haven in the bustling city. Teena and Sarah are sitting together, the clinking of ice blending with distant city noises.

Sarah's voice is slurred as she playfully teases Teena, "Tomorrow, we should slow down with the drinking; it's affecting my work."

Teena smiles, her eyes mischievous. "Not me. I find pleasure in it, and no hangovers either."

Sarah leans in, her voice teasing yet sincere. "I bet you still can't get John out of your heart; that's why you can't paint like before."

Teena's face softens, and she nods. "Yes, you're right. You always understand me so well. I'm already obsessed."

Sarah's expression turns serious, her voice filled with concern. "He's your sister's husband, Teena. This is a mistake. It might lead to more complications."

Teena's voice rises, defiant and raw. "I don't care. I can't help how I feel. It's like he's always on my mind."

Sarah's voice softens, her eyes filled with compassion. "Teena, you need to let go. It's not healthy to hold on to these feelings."

Teena sighs, her voice filled with longing and loss. "I know, but I can't help it. Seeing them together just reminds me of what I lost."

Sarah puts a hand on her shoulder, her voice gentle and encouraging. "You haven't lost anything, Teena. You still have your talent and your future ahead of you."

Teena looks down, her voice breaking. "It's just hard, Sarah. I feel like a part of me will always be incomplete."

Sarah's voice is soothing as she reassures her friend. "It's okay to feel that way, but you need to focus on yourself and your art. Don't let this consume you."

Teena nods, knowing Sarah is right, but the pain in her heart lingers. Their conversation turns serious, and they probe the intricacies of love, loss, and self-discovery, framed by the locations that are as much a part of the story as the characters themselves.

Their conversation becomes uneasy, and an uncomfortable silence fills the air.

The film studio in Los Angeles is abuzz with activity. Technicians, artists, and assistants dart around, working in a choreographed frenzy. John, looking dashing and full of anticipation for his scenes, is suddenly pulled aside by the director.

The director's face is apologetic as he breaks the news. "John, I'm afraid we have to postpone the shoot. Your co-artist Mia has come down with a complicated viral fever. She won't be able to shoot for at least two months."

John's eyes widen, and a feeling of disappointment washes over him. "What? Two months? But we've already shot half of the combination scenes!"

"I know, it's unfortunate," the director says, his voice filled with genuine regret. "But Mia's health comes first, and we can't proceed without her."

John sighs, his shoulders slumping. He understands the situation, but the delay stings nonetheless. The excitement in the studio gives way to a subdued atmosphere as the news spreads, and John's thoughts drift, reflecting on the unpredictability of the world.

Meanwhile, thousands of miles away, in New York, on Sarah's terrace, Teena, Reena, and Sarah are gathered, the city's distant sounds creating a gentle backdrop. Their drinks are in moderation tonight, the mood more somber and reflective.

With sincere concern in her eyes, Sarah turns to Teena. "Teena, I still think you should consider talking to a psychiatrist about your feelings."

Teena's face clouds with reluctance. "I don't know, Sarah. It's not easy for me."

Sarah's voice is gentle, her words chosen with care. "I understand, but it might help you process everything and move forward."

Teena sighs, her gaze drifting to the sparkling lights of the city. The suggestion weighs heavily on her mind. "Maybe you're right."

Sarah reaches out, her touch reassuring. "And don't forget to confess in church too. It can be cathartic, and it might bring you some peace."

Teena's eyes meet Sarah's, the uncertainty in them beginning to give way to consideration. Sarah's advice, though challenging, resonates, and Teena knows she must take steps to heal.

Together, they continue their conversation, the terrace a sanctuary where secrets are shared, advice is offered, and the bonds of friendship are strengthened. The night wears on, each woman drawing strength from the others, united by their shared experiences and hopes for the future.

John returns to his and Reena's cozy living room, his shoulders slumped, and his usually vibrant eyes clouded with frustration. Reena, engaged in arranging fresh flowers on a table, senses his disappointment even before she turns to look at him. Her heart aches at the sight of him, and she drops what she's doing to attend to him.

"What happened, John?" she asks softly, concern evident in her eyes. "Why do you look so upset?"

John rubs his forehead, the lines of stress creasing his face as he explains, "The shoot got postponed for two months. Our co-artist is unwell, and we can't continue without her."

Reena steps closer, her eyes full of sympathy, and gently places a hand on his arm. Her touch is warm and soothing. "I'm sorry to hear that, but I'm sure everything will work out fine. We just need to be patient."

John looks at her, slightly reassured by her faith in him, and nods. "Yeah, you're right. It's just frustrating to wait."

Reena embraces John, her arms wrapping around him tenderly. She understands his passion and commitment to his work and feels his pain. Her touch is reassuring, comforting him in a way that only she can. John's body relaxes into her embrace, the frustration slowly ebbing away, replaced by a sense of peace and connection.

Meanwhile, in a completely different setting, the psychiatrist's office in the heart of New York offers a comfortable, safe space. Decorated with calming colors and soft lighting, it's a sanctuary for those seeking help. Teena sits nervously in a plush chair, the weight of her emotions palpable, her hands clasped tightly in her lap.

Dr. Patel, a middle-aged man with a kind face, sits across from her, his eyes soft, his demeanor encouraging trust. "Take your time, Teena," he says softly, his voice gentle. "You can share whatever you're comfortable with."

Teena's voice breaks, her eyes looking down as she begins to open up. "Doctor, I... I can't stop thinking about someone. It's like he's always on my mind, and I can't get over the memories we shared. It's painful, and I feel this overwhelming possessiveness towards him."

Dr. Patel's eyes are empathetic; he recognizes the complexity of Teena's feelings. His voice is gentle as he responds, "It seems like you're experiencing a form of obsessive-compulsive disorder (OCD) related to romantic thoughts.

These persistent, unwanted thoughts can be distressing, I understand."

"Yes, exactly," Teena whispers, her voice quivering. "I can't seem to control it, and it's affecting my daily life."

The doctor's face is encouraging as he leans forward, "It's essential to remember that you're not alone in this, Teena. Such feelings are not uncommon, and there are ways to address them. We can work together to help you manage these emotions."

As he explains various treatments, Teena's face shifts from despair to hope. Her body language changes, and her shoulders straighten, reflecting her newfound determination.

"Thank you, Doctor," she says, her voice now resolute. "I'm willing to do whatever it takes to move past this phase and find peace."

"That's the spirit, Teena," Dr. Patel responds sincerely, a supportive smile gracing his lips. "Remember, healing takes time, but with patience and dedication, you'll get there."

Teena leaves the psychiatrist's office with renewed vigor, a spark in her eyes that wasn't there before. She's ready to face her struggles, determined to rebuild her life, and find the peace she so desperately seeks. The door closes behind her, leaving Dr. Patel to reflect on the progress made, hopeful for her future.

The regular buzz of the office is broken by a palpable change in the atmosphere as Mr. Anderson, the usually unflappable boss, enters. His demeanor today is softened, a strange departure from his usual stubborn and authoritative presence. Staff members look up from their work, their eyes widening and following him as he moves past them without his customary brisk pleasantries. He heads straight to his cabin, his shoulders slightly hunched, his steps less confident. Whispers and exchanged glances fill the room as everyone senses the change in his demeanor.

His face, which is often set in a determined expression, now wears a different, more troubled look. As he closes his office door with uncharacteristic gentleness, the sound seems to echo through the room, leaving a lingering silence. He isolates himself from the rest, a sense of unease settling in the office.

Reena, sensitive to emotions, feels something amiss. Her concern for Mr. Anderson leads her to approach his office, her steps hesitant. Her hand trembles as she knocks gently on the door, her voice tinged with genuine worry, "Mr. Anderson, is everything alright?"

His response comes through the door, his voice betraying a hint of vulnerability that Reena has never heard before. "Leave me alone for some time, Reena."

The words hit Reena like a physical blow. She's taken aback by the tone, her heart aching with concern and confusion. She returns to her desk, unable to shake the feeling that something profound has changed. The staff members exchange concerned looks, their curiosity and worry piqued by Mr. Anderson's uncharacteristic behavior.

Meanwhile, at a local church, the soft light filters through the stained-glass windows, casting a warm, ethereal glow over the pews. The serene atmosphere embraces Teena as she enters, her face pale, her eyes reflecting her inner turmoil.

She approaches a confessional booth, her hands clasped tightly together, the heavy, polished wood standing as a gateway to solace and guidance. Taking a deep breath to steady herself, she begins to speak to the priest within, her voice trembling with raw emotion, "Father, I... I can't control my feelings. I've developed an overwhelming obsession with a married man."

The priest listens attentively, his unseen presence a comforting anchor. His voice is kindly, full of understanding, as he responds, "My child, human emotions can be complex and challenging to navigate. Remember that every one of us faces trials, and we're called to support one another."

Teena feels a lump in her throat as she listens to the priest's gentle words. They flow over her like a soothing balm, easing her wounded soul.

He continues, his voice gentle and reassuring, "Focus on nurturing healthy relationships and cultivating love and kindness in your heart. Letting go of obsessions can be difficult, but with faith and determination, you can overcome them."

The confession session continues, and as the priest's words sink in, Teena's shoulders begin to relax. The tension she carried with her started to dissipate. When she leaves the confessional booth, her steps are lighter, her face reflecting a sense of relief and renewed purpose.

The church door closes behind her, leaving a silence filled with hope and redemption. Both the office and the church become symbols of transformation and understanding, places where personal battles are faced, and inner demons confronted.

Chapter 8.

A few days later, Teena's apartment is shrouded in silence, the only illumination coming from a dim lamp on her desk. She sits hunched over her creative work, her eyes intense, her hand trembling as she sketches. Her art, usually a refuge, now feels like a battleground, each line a struggle to capture the chaos of her emotions.

The room bears the scars of her mental battle; discarded sketches litter her desk, each attempt falling short, never quite reaching the essence of what she's feeling. Frustration mounts within her, growing like a storm.

Later, Teena sits on the edge of her bed, lost in the shadows of her mind. The room, bathed in moonlight, feels both calming and haunting. Sleep eludes her; her mind is a whirlpool of uncontrolled obsession and guilt.

She clutches a small bottle of pills, her fingers tracing its contours, her mind grappling with the idea of medication as a solution to a problem that feels beyond her control. Memories of the priest's words, the doctor's counsel, and John's face intermingle in a confusing dance.

Her face twists in conflict as she battles the uninvited feelings for John, her beloved sister's husband. The reality that it's wrong on every level torments her, but the feelings refuse to be silenced.

With a sudden burst of determination, Teena thrusts the bottle of pills into a drawer. Her eyes are wild, her breathing heavy. She retrieves an outline painting of John's face, her hands shaking.

Her eyes lock onto the image, and for a moment, she's lost in a world where her feelings for John are acceptable. A world where love isn't a torment. The room seems to pulse with her emotions, the boundaries between right and wrong blurring.

Conflicted, she walks over to the fireplace, the painting in her hands feeling both like a treasure and a curse. She holds it over the flames, hesitating, her heart pounding.

With a painful cry, she lets the flames consume the painting. Her face is a canvas of agony, relief, and a desperate need to be free. The flames reduce the painting to ashes, symbolic of her attempt to burn away an obsession she never wanted.

Teena stands before the fireplace, the ashes a haunting reminder of her struggle. She closes her eyes, tears escaping, a mixture of grief for what was lost and hope for what could be gained.

She knows this is a step towards healing, but the path ahead is still uncertain. The room returns to silence, a silence filled with the echoes of a battle fought within the human heart.

John is seated on the couch in Reena's living room, his phone in hand, concern etched across his face. He dials a number, his heart heavy with worry.

"Mia, how are you feeling?" he asks, his voice tinged with concern. "Heard you've been under the weather."

Hey, John," Mia's voice comes through the phone, weak and faltering. "Yeah, I've got a fever. Doc says it's goanna be a couple of weeks, and they've suggested absolute rest for a month'.

"I'm really sorry to hear that," John replies, genuine sympathy in his tone. "Take care of yourself, okay? Wishing you a speedy recovery."

"Thanks, John. I appreciate it," Mia responds gratitude in her voice.

The scene shifts to Reena, strolling along a serene beach, her puppy bounding joyfully beside her. The waves lap gently at the shore, creating a soothing rhythm. Her mind is lost in thought, her eyes reflecting the tranquility of the scene.

Without warning, the peacefulness is shattered by a loud gunshot, the sound echoing ominously through the air. A bullet whizzes past Reena's head, and terror grips her as she bolts towards home, her heart pounding, her mind filled with dread.

Elsewhere in the city, James, an investigative journalist, walks briskly down a busy street, his eyes glued to his phone. The world around him fades into a blur as he navigates the labyrinth of the city.

Chapter 9.

A sudden CRASH pulls him from his thoughts as a bullet narrowly misses him, shattering a nearby car window. Fear overtakes him, and he runs, ducking into an alleyway, his mind reeling, his body driven by survival.

In a tranquil park, Lily, another journalist, is absorbed in her jog, her body moving rhythmically, her mind lost in the freedom of movement. The serenity is ripped away by a sharp CRACK, and a bullet pierces a tree just inches from her.

Time seems to stand still as she stares, frozen, at the splintered wood. Then, instinct takes over, and she runs, her breath coming in ragged gasps, her heart racing with terror.

On a rooftop overlooking the city, Mark, the third journalist, stands captivated by the view, his camera clicking as he captures the essence of the cityscape. His world is reduced to the frame of his lens, the city unfolding before him.

A sudden bullet strike breaks his concentration, and he's thrown into chaos as dust and fragments fill the air. Fear propels him to the ground, and he scrambles for cover, his body shaking, his mind a whirlwind of confusion.

In the dark corners of the city, shadows lengthen, and whispers of danger grow. The echoes of gunshots linger, the characters' fear is palpable. A mystery begins to unfold, danger lurking just out of sight, tension building. The lives of these individuals have been irrevocably altered, pulled into a web of intrigue and uncertainty. The day's events weigh heavily, leaving them to ponder their fate as the world continues to turn, indifferent to their fears.

Rain begins to fall slowly on Sarah's terrace, casting a soft and reflective sheen over the city. The distant lights glisten through the raindrops, a serene backdrop to the tension building between Teena and Sarah as they stand facing each other, expressions tense.

"You've changed so much, Teena," Sarah teases. "What happened to the calm and gentle girl I met years ago?"

"People change, Sarah," Teena replies bitterly. "Life isn't stagnant, and neither am I."

As the rain picks up, Sarah's concern grows. "But this change is different. You've become consumed by something, something dangerous. This obsession with your sister's husband..."

"You don't understand, Sarah," Teena snaps defensively. "None of your advice, nor the psychiatrist's, nor even the priest's, has helped."

The rain intensifies, reflecting the rising tension between them. "Maybe it's time we put an end to this friendship. From tomorrow, we're strangers," Sarah declares, firm and unyielding.

Teena's desperation becomes palpable. "Sarah, please, you're the only one who truly understands me. I can't lose you."

"I can't continue this friendship, Teena," Sarah says, sadness in her voice.

"You've crossed all limits. Your obsession is tearing you apart and affecting everyone around you, especially your sister's marriage," Sarah accuses.

The rain turns into a downpour, mirroring Teena's emotional turmoil. "You don't understand, Sarah. Please, don't do anything that will ruin my sister's happiness."

Teena's grip on Sarah's wrists is frantic, unyielding. Fear widens Sarah's eyes. "Let go, Teena!" she cries.

In a blind, impulsive moment, Teena pushes Sarah away. The momentum carries Sarah to the edge of the terrace, her feet slipping on the now-soaked surface. Time freezes as Sarah's body tilts backward over the railing. Her eyes lock with Teena's, filled with a silent scream, before she falls.

"Sarah! No!" Teena shrieks, her voice raw and horrified.

Teena is next seen in a hospital, pale and shaken, sitting in a chair. Police officers take her statement, and doctors attend to Sarah's lifeless body.

"She... she slipped. It was an accident," Teena stammers, her voice a hollow whisper.

Later, Teena stands alone in a hospital corridor. The rain still pours outside, mirroring her internal chaos. The weight of what transpired settles upon her, leaving her lost and broken. A whisper escapes her lips, a single word filled with grief, guilt, and loss:

"Sarah..."

The tension was palpable as Anderson's office filled with an assembly of the intrepid investigative journalists, Reena, James, Lily, and Mark, their families, and several police officers. Their faces were etched with concern and determination, a stark reminder of the high stakes they were facing.

Reena, the leader of the group, exuded strength, her posture upright, her chin held high, yet her eyes betrayed a tumult of emotions. They sparkled with determination but were shadowed by the immense weight of responsibility that rested on her shoulders.

The door swung open, and Anderson, their mentor, and guide, entered the room. His face was a complex canvas, concern and resolve mingling in his eyes, his lips pressed tightly together. He surveyed the room, his gaze lingering on each face before he spoke, his voice tinged with solemnity.

"Thank you all for being here," he began, his voice quivering. "What happened today was an attempt on our lives. Four close encounters with death cannot be ignored."

A murmur went through the room, and families of the journalists exchanged worried glances. The danger was no longer an abstraction; it was real, it was close, and it had touched them all.

Tears welled in Anderson's eyes as he continued, "They targeted my wife, and they warned me next it would be you. I hesitated to air the news we've uncovered. I feared for your safety."

John, Reena's husband, reached out to gently squeeze her hand, a silent reassurance amid the turmoil.

"But we can't let fear dictate our actions," Anderson declared, his voice gaining strength. "We've collected evidence that exposes one of the biggest scams in our nation's history. The truth needs to come out."

The room was charged with a renewed sense of purpose. James, Lily, and Mark exchanged determined glances, their commitment to their cause unshaken.

"We won't be intimidated. We've faced dangers before. This won't stop us,"

James asserted.

"Our duty is to the truth and the public. We can't back down," Lily added firmly.

"They may try to silence us, but they can't erase what we know," Mark concluded, his voice steady and calm.

Reena stepped forward, her voice unwavering, her eyes reflecting an indomitable spirit. "We're prepared for the risks. If they're willing to kill us to stop the truth, then so be it. Our duty is greater."

Anderson's eyes filled with pride and a hint of concern as he listened to his team's commitment. "Remember, we all have families, and responsibilities. We must take precautions."

"We know that, Mr. Anderson. We've considered the consequences," Reena assured him.

Silence fell over the room as they collectively absorbed the magnitude of their decision. The stakes were clear, the path fraught with danger, but the resolve was unwavering.

"Let's wait for the police investigation. They've assured us protection. We'll face this together," Anderson said gravely.

The group nodded in agreement, their solidarity evident in their shared purpose. The truth was their weapon, and they were ready to wield it, no matter the cost. In that room, at that moment, they were bound together by a cause greater than themselves, ready to face whatever lay ahead.

The somber notes of the final farewell lingered in the air as the mourners dispersed from Sarah's funeral. Among them, Teena sat isolated and adrift in a quiet corner, her face as expressionless as a still pond, her eyes a void where emotions were carefully guarded.

"I lost a real good friend..." she reflected, her voice a soft murmur that only she could hear.

Her mind was a whirlpool of confusion and guilt. The memory of the accidental push, the horrifying scream, Sarah's lifeless body – all replayed in her mind like a relentless nightmare. And the police had not taken her seriously as a prime suspect. Was it luck or a curse?

As Teena drove back to her apartment in the bustling heart of New York City, the car's interior seemed to close in on her. The radio crackled to life, announcing the sniper attack on the journalists, one of whom was Reena, her own flesh and blood. The news sent a shockwave through her, her heart pounding in her chest like a wild drum.

"This is much more dangerous than I thought..." she whispered to herself, pulling over by the side of the road, her hands trembling on the steering wheel.

Her mind raced with images of Reena, so strong, so fearless, facing dangers that Teena had never imagined. With a deep breath, she dialed Reena's number, her voice laced with anxiety.

"Hello, my dear," Reena answered, her voice a soothing balm.

"How are you so cool about all this?" Teena stammered, her voice breaking. "It's not the first time. Earlier, they warned, dashed our car... I haven't even told John or you... My passion for investigative journalism overcame me... and we're exceptional daring genes, not only identical in everything but also in facing life's challenges... we possess the same courage," Reena explained, her words firm yet comforting.

Teena's heart ached with a mix of admiration and a strange, growing resolve. "You dared for a cause... I am dared to get your man..." she thought, her inner voice a whisper filled with determination and guilt.

Her decision was quick, her purpose clear. "I need to see you. I'll be flying to your town," she said, her voice resolute.

The connection with Reena ended, but the weight of the emotions lingered. Teena sat in the car, her mind a storm of thoughts and feelings. She was on the brink of a journey, not just to another town but into the depths of her own soul. With the intensity of emotions guiding her, she set forth, ready to face whatever lay ahead.

At that moment, the city's noise faded into the background, and all that mattered was the path she had chosen. A path filled with uncertainty, courage, and a desperate need to right the wrongs of the past. The road stretched ahead, and Teena faced it with a newfound determination, propelled by the complexity of her emotions and the unbreakable bond with her sister.

Teena flew to Carmel, the journey filled with anticipation and an undercurrent of trepidation. Arriving at Reena and John's home, she was greeted by familiar faces and a cozy atmosphere. The dining room was illuminated by the warm glow of the lights, offering a picture of domestic bliss as Reena, John, and their playful puppy gathered around the dinner table.

"You know, Anderson and the others were really brave today," Reena said, smiling, her eyes sparkling with admiration. "Despite the threats, they're still determined to uncover the truth."

John looked up, concern etching his face. "It's a dangerous path they're treading, Reena. I just hope they stay safe."

Reena's response was resolute, her voice firm. "They're doing it for a cause, John. We can't let fear hold us back."

As the conversation flowed, Teena's mind was elsewhere. Her eyes kept drifting to John, her heart betraying her thoughts. The puppy scampered around the table, a bundle of energy, drawing a smile from Teena. "Hey there, little one. You're just full of energy, aren't you?" she said, her voice softening.

Seemingly oblivious to her hidden emotions, John laughed. "Seems like our furry friend missed you too."

Teena turned the conversation to John's work, her interest feigned but her gaze intent. "So, John, how's your AD shoot going?"

John took a sip of water, his eyes meeting hers. "Well, it's on hold for now. My co-artist fell ill with a severe viral infection, so we have to wait for her recovery before resuming."

"That's unfortunate," Reena chimed in, showing genuine interest. "But I'm sure it'll pick up once she's better."

The dinner continued with light-hearted conversations, yet an undercurrent of tension remained. It was unspoken but palpable, lurking beneath the surface of their shared laughter and stories.

Later that night, Teena sat on the edge of the bed, her face reflecting the turmoil within her. The room was still, the puppy asleep, oblivious to her restless contemplation. Her thoughts were a storm, her mind a battlefield of conflicting emotions.

"How do I make him mine? How do I replace Reena?" she wondered, her voice a mere whisper in her mind. "These thoughts are consuming me, driving me mad."

The idea took shape slowly, insidiously. It crept into her consciousness, taking root, and growing stronger. "Sarah's accident was an accident, but what if I plan it perfectly? If I can remove Reena from the picture, make it look like an accident too, the police will surely focus their investigation in that direction."

Her eyes narrowed as she entertained the idea, her thoughts racing, her heart pounding. A plan began to unfold, meticulous and sinister.

"If I can create the illusion of danger for Reena, maybe even frame it as another attempt on the journalists' lives, it could be the perfect opportunity to eliminate her," she mused, her fingers nervously clenching the edge of the bedspread. "I have to be careful, meticulous. I can't afford any mistakes this time."

The pieces of her plan fell into place, guided by determination and an unsettling calmness. Teena's mind was clear, her path chosen. It was a dark path, fraught with danger and deception, but she was ready to tread it, her eyes fixed on her goal, her heart resolute.

"Reena's demise will appear to be a tragic accident, a result of the same dangerous circumstances that targeted the journalists," she thought, her eyes gleaming with a newfound purpose. "It will be a masterful illusion, one that no one will see through. I'll make sure of it."

Chapter 10.

Her decision was made, her course set. The night deepened, and Teena lay awake, the weight of her choice heavy on her soul. But there was no turning back. The game had begun, and she was all in, ready to play her hand, no matter the cost.

Anderson sat at his desk, his brow furrowed with concern, his fingers drumming a nervous rhythm on the wooden surface. The room was filled with the faint scent of old books and coffee, but Anderson's mind was elsewhere. He stared at the evidence board, lost in thought, the web of connections and leads taunting him from the wall. The phone buzzed, breaking his concentration, and he picked it up, his heart pounding.

"Inspector, I appreciate your efforts to provide protection for my team," he said, his voice strained. "But it seems they're not willing to accept it."

"I understand, Mr. Anderson," came the reply, the Inspector's voice filled with understanding. "It's not uncommon for people to be wary of constant surveillance. But we can't guarantee their safety if they refuse protection."

Anderson's frustration bubbled to the surface. "I know, I know. It's just... these are my most trusted journalists. They've faced danger before, but this is different. They're up against something powerful, something dangerous."

The Inspector's voice softened, his words sympathetic. "I sympathize with your concern, but they need to understand the gravity of the situation. If they don't accept protection, there's only so much we can do."

Resigned, Anderson ran a hand through his hair. "I'll talk to them again. Try to convince them. But I can't force them to do something they're not comfortable with."

"We'll be here if they change their minds, Mr. Anderson. Their safety is our priority."

"Thank you, Inspector," Anderson said softly, the weight of responsibility heavy on his shoulders. "I hope they realize the risks they're taking."

At Reena's home that night, Reena, James, Lily, and Mark sat around a table, the room bathed in the soft glow of a single lamp. The evidence and photographs were spread before them, the faces of those involved staring back with cold indifference.

"We can't let fear dictate our actions," Reena declared, her eyes ablaze with determination. "We've faced threats before, and we're not about to back down now."

James nodded, his jaw set. "I agree. Our duty is to the truth, no matter what."

Lily's voice trembled, her eyes wide with concern. "But what about the danger? We can't ignore it."

"I get it," Mark said, his voice thoughtful, "but we can't compromise our integrity either."

Reena looked at each of them, her eyes searching, her heart swelling with pride. "Look, I know it's risky, but let's stick together. We won't let fear control us."

Back in Anderson's office the next day, he sat back in his chair, the memory of his conversation with the Inspector still echoing in his mind. His team was fiercely independent, dedicated to their cause. They were a stubborn bunch, but their tenacity was what made them great journalists.

He leaned forward, determination burning in his eyes, his soul filled with resolve.

"I won't force them into protection," he vowed, his voice resolute. "But I'll do everything in my power to keep them safe."

His words lingered in the silence, a solemn promise, a declaration of his commitment to his team. The road ahead was fraught with danger, but Anderson knew he would face it head-on, for the sake of truth and justice.

Reena's home was unnervingly quiet as Teena stepped out of the shower. The call bell rang, its sharp chime breaking the stillness of the house. She wrapped herself in a towel, curiosity piqued, and made her way to the door.

John's face, flushed with embarrassment, greeted her as the door swung open. His eyes widened at her state of undress, his mind reeling from the sudden intimacy of the moment. He tried to look away, to move to the sanctuary of his bedroom, but Teena's grip was strong and unyielding.

Her eyes sparkled with mischief, her smile knowing and tantalizing. The towel fell to the floor, and she pulled him close, her skin warm and inviting. John's resistance crumbled, his self-control slipping through his fingers like sand.

Rational thought gave way to primal desire, his mind a whirlpool of confusion and longing.

Afterward, shame washed over John like a cold wave, his body trembling with remorse and confusion. He couldn't bear to look at Teena, her satisfied smile a sharp contrast to his deepening despair. Escape was the only option, and he rushed to the beachside, the salty air doing little to clear his muddled thoughts.

Teena's smile lingered, a triumphant glow in her eyes. She knew she had him now, a pawn in her intricate game. The beach called to her, the lure of John's distress too enticing to resist.

As she approached the shoreline, John's hunched figure came into view. He looked small, his shoulders slumped, his face etched with regret. The waves crashed against the shore, a rhythmic reminder of the unstoppable force of human nature.

"If I were to tell this to sis Reena, what's your position? Could you convince her?" Teena's voice was light, almost teasing, but her eyes were sharp.

John's voice broke, the weight of his mistake crushing him. "I'm sorry. I made a big mistake. I lost my senses for a few minutes. Please don't tell Reena. It would disrupt our married life. Let it be."

Teena's laughter was musical, her delight in his misery clear. "I know you want me too. That's why you enjoyed the ultimate real sex with me," she taunted. "I can't promise you that. I might use this information when the right time comes."

John's face paled, his mind reeling from the realization of his vulnerability. Teena's words were a knife to his heart, a cold reminder of the power she now wielded over him. The sun dipped low on the horizon, casting a golden glow over the beach, but John felt nothing but darkness closing in.

He knew he had lost, his momentary lapse of control a fatal mistake. Teena had won, her smile triumphant, her victory complete.

The night was filled with shadows, a gentle hum of the living room's air conditioner the only sound as Teena sat hunched over her laptop. Her eyes were hungry, filled with an insidious determination that was entirely new to her. This was a world she had never ventured into before, a game she was learning to play.

Her fingers danced across the keyboard, her search taking her to the darkest corners of the web. Information on accidents, mishaps, and things that could happen to anyone but had a lingering taste of possibility. She was no professional killer, no master of espionage; just a young woman with a twisted desire and a mind willing to explore it.

"If I can find the right scenario, it'll be the perfect cover. Something that won't raise suspicions," she muttered to herself, her voice barely a whisper. Her breath caught as she found a list of natural accidents, her mind racing with possibilities.

The scenarios unfolded in her head, images of Reena's daily routines and habits merging with these accidents. A slip in the bathroom, a stumble on the stairs, a gas leak – all things that could happen, all things that would not look out of place.

"It has to be something that she wouldn't question, something that could easily happen to anyone," Teena whispered, her voice filled with dark excitement. Her mind was working in ways she had never thought possible, the moral barriers breaking down as her plans took shape.

Teena's heart pounded as she realized what she was capable of. This wasn't a game anymore; it was a deadly dance, a series of moves and countermoves that had to be perfectly executed. Her thoughts were consumed with timing, precision, and understanding every aspect of Reena's life to make the plan work.

She was alone with her darkness, the familiar surroundings of Reena's home taking on a sinister edge as her planning continued. Hours slipped by, her research growing more and more detailed. Maps, schedules, weather patterns – everything was considered, and everything was analyzed.

"This has to work. It's the only way to remove her from the picture without raising suspicions," Teena said, her voice filled with conviction. The words hung in the air, a chilling testament to her resolve.

She looked at her reflection in the darkened window, her face pale, her eyes wide with both fear and anticipation. This was a new Teena, a person she had never thought she would become. But the path was laid out now, the plans were in motion, and there was no turning back.

Teena's thoughts were cold, calculated, and devoid of emotion. She knew what she was doing was wrong, but the thrill of the plan, the allure of the unknown, was too strong to resist.

The night wore on, the room filled with the soft glow of the laptop and the relentless clicking of keys. Teena's mind was sharp, her resolve unwavering. She was playing a dangerous game, a game she was willing to win at any cost.

The morning was still and quiet, the park filled with the gentle rustle of leaves and the distant chatter of birds. It was a seemingly ordinary day, but for Teena, it was the day her plan would come to fruition. Her heart pounded in her chest as she observed Reena's familiar form, walking along a path near the edge of the park. Everything was ready, every detail meticulously prepared. This was her moment.

As Reena continued her leisurely stroll, Teena's fingers reached into her pocket, gripping the remote that controlled the carefully rigged branch overhead. Her breath caught in her throat as she watched Reena's every move, timing it perfectly.

The seconds ticked by like hours, Teena's mind a whirlwind of anticipation and fear. Then, as if guided by some dark force, her thumb pressed the button.

The sound of cracking wood filled the air as the branch came crashing down, a deadly missile aimed directly at Reena. Teena's eyes widened, her heart aching with a strange mix of excitement and terror. But then, in a split second, something incredible happened.

Reena, sensing the danger, dove to the side with a grace that was almost supernatural. The branch missed her by mere inches, her body hitting the ground with a thud. Teena's breath caught in her throat, disbelief and shock washing over her.

"No... it can't be. How did she escape that?" she whispered, her voice trembling. Her mind was a storm of confusion and frustration, her plan crumbling before her very eyes.

Reena, still on the ground, quickly assessed her surroundings, suspicion and confusion etched across her face. She knew something wasn't right, something more than a simple accident. Her eyes narrowed as she scanned the distance, unknowingly locking onto Teena's hiding spot.

Teena, her mind reeling, retreated from her hiding place, a sense of panic rising within her. Her plan had been perfect, every detail accounted for, every variable considered. And yet, Reena had escaped. It was as if fate itself had intervened, a cruel twist that left Teena's world spinning.

"This... this wasn't supposed to happen. How did she escape my perfectly executed plan?" she whispered, her voice filled with disbelief and disappointment. Her body felt heavy, her determination shattered by the miraculous escape.

Teena's mind raced, struggling to comprehend what had happened. Her perfect plan had failed, and she was left with nothing but questions and doubt. Had she missed something? Had Reena known? Was there something more to this that she couldn't see?

"This changes everything... What am I missing? How did she know?" Teena murmured, her voice breaking. The weight of failure weighed heavily on her, a bitter taste that lingered long after the moment had passed.

As Reena walked away, still clutching her sore elbow, Teena was left standing in the shadows, her mind a dark and tangled mess. The game had changed, and she was no longer in control. Her perfect plan had unraveled, and she was left with nothing but the cold, hard truth that she was not as clever as she thought.

At that moment, Teena realized that she was playing with forces beyond her understanding, a dangerous dance that could consume her. Her lack of experience, her naivety, had been exposed, and she was left with a stark choice: abandon her dark path or embrace it, knowing that the stakes had never been higher.

Anderson sat at his desk, his brow furrowed in concern. The office was filled with a tension that was almost tangible. He listened intently, his hands clasped tightly, as his staff recounted the details of Reena's near accident. His thoughts were a whirlwind of worry and confusion. "Another close call," he sighed heavily. "Are they targeting her specifically?" His words echoed the fear in his eyes.

His staff members exchanged worried glances, understanding the gravity of the situation. They all felt it, a shared dread that chilled the room. "It seems that way, Anderson," one of them finally nodded. "And this time, Reena wasn't so lucky. She managed to avoid the danger, but it's getting too close for comfort." The words were spoken softly but carried a heavy weight.

A mixture of frustration and determination was visible on Anderson's face. "We can't let this continue. We must put an end to this, now. I will not risk your lives any further," he declared, his voice rising with conviction. His staff nodded in agreement, a shared determination to uncover the truth. Their faces were set, and the decision was made. Something had to be done.

Chapter 11.

In the exterior of a hospital. Reena, John, and Teena were exiting the building. Reena's arm was in a sling, but she looked remarkably composed. They headed towards a waiting car, their faces a mixture of relief and concern.

Reena got into the driver's seat, John beside her, and Teena in the back seat. The car started moving, the engine's hum a subdued background to their thoughts.

"Thanks for coming with us, Teena," Reena said, glancing at her. "It's been a crazy day."

Teena's gaze was distant, lost in thought as she looked out of the window. "Yeah, crazy," she said softly, her voice barely above a whisper.

Reena shot a concerned look at Teena, sensing something amiss. "Hey, you're awfully quiet back there. Everything alright?" she teased, trying to lighten the mood.

Teena's forced smile didn't quite reach her eyes. "Yeah, everything's fine," she replied, her hesitation betraying her words.

Reena exchanged a quick glance with John, sensing that Teena wasn't being entirely truthful. "Alright, if you say so," she said softly, letting the matter drop.

Teena let out a sigh, her mind still grappling with the events of the day. How did Reena manage to escape? Sarah's accident was so easy, but this... this was different. Something wasn't adding up.

As the car pulled into the driveway of Reena's home, the mood ended with a lingering sense of unease, an unspoken suspicion that hung heavily in the air. The weight of it was palpable, a silent reminder that something was very, very wrong.

The cozy living room was bathed in a warm glow, casting gentle shadows on the walls. Reena rested her head on John's lap, finding comfort in his presence. Her arm ached, but it was nothing compared to the pain in her heart. Teena, feeling out of place, occupied another sofa, her company a small, playful puppy. A moment of tranquility hung in the air, a stark contrast to the chaos of the day.

"Reena," John whispered, his fingers gently stroking her hair. "You've been through so much. I can't bear to see you facing these challenges anymore. It's time to consider quitting this job, love. I can't stand the thought of you in danger."

Reena looked up at him, her eyes filled with affection. "Don't worry, my dear. I'm strong, and I know what I'm doing. This is my passion, and I won't give it up easily."

John's eyes were clouded with worry, his love for Reena evident in every line of his face. "But the danger is real, Reena. I can't keep living in fear for you."

She reached up, cupping his cheek. "I promise I'll be careful. I won't take unnecessary risks."

He sighed, the sound heavy with emotion. "You're a force to be reckoned with, I know. But my heart aches every time you're out there facing danger."

Reena's smile was teasing, her eyes sparkling. "Don't worry, my dear. If anything were to happen to me, you still have my twin soul, Teena. She can take my place as the wife of John."

The words hung in the air, a joke that carried more weight than she intended.

Teena's heart skipped a beat, her mind reeling from Reena's unexpected words. John's face tensed as he processed the statement.

"Reena," he stammered, visibly shocked. "What are you saying? If anything ever happened to you, I would never marry again. My love for you is so strong that I can't even imagine another woman in my life."

Reena's eyes widened, filled with a mix of surprise and deep emotion. She reached up to cup John's face, her voice soft. "Oh, John, your commitment to me is beyond words. I love you more than anything."

"And I you, Reena," he whispered, his voice filled with earnest love. "You're irreplaceable. You're my one and only."

Their lips met in a passionate kiss, a testament to a love that defied all odds. Teena watched from her spot on the sofa, a mix of awe and guilt swirling within her.

"What have I done?" she whispered to herself. "John's commitment to Reena is unbreakable. His love is exceptional."

As Reena and John continued to share their love, Teena's heart ached with guilt. She realized the depth of the consequences her actions may have on their lives, and a lingering sense of unease settled over her.

Reena and John returned to their conversation, but Teena's thoughts lingered on John's words. His love was extraordinary, a force that seemed unbreakable.

As the evening wore on, Teena's thoughts churned. She knew that the path she'd chosen was fraught with risk, and the consequences of her actions loomed large. But John's love for Reena was a beacon, a testament to the power of devotion and fidelity.

The weight of her choices pressed heavily upon her, and she knew that the road ahead was uncertain. But one thing was clear: the love between Reena and John was exceptional, a love that would endure anything.

The evening had settled over the town, and the interior of Anderson's office was filled with an atmosphere charged with anticipation and weighty decisions. Anderson stood behind his desk, addressing the press that packed the room. His voice rang loud and clear, echoing the urgency of the moment.

"Ladies and gentlemen, esteemed members of the media," he began, his eyes sweeping the room, "Today marks a pivotal moment in our journey to uncover the truth. Our pursuit of justice has led us down a perilous path, riddled with obstacles and threats that have tested our resolve."

His voice dropped to a somber tone, the weight of his words sinking in. "However, in light of recent developments and the safety of our dedicated team, we have reached a difficult but necessary decision. Our commitment to truth and transparency remains unwavering, but we also must recognize the reality of the risks we face."

The reporters leaned in, their pens poised, sensing the gravity of the announcement. Anderson continued, his voice commanding attention, "Our investigation has unearthed critical information that strikes at the heart of power dynamics and secrets that many wish to remain buried. Our intentions have always been rooted in integrity, but we cannot ignore the dangers that have emerged, threatening the very lives of those who seek to shed light on the darkness."

A heavy silence followed as he raised a firm hand, his expression resolute, "The responsibility I carry for my team's safety is paramount. Journalism is a beacon of democracy, but it cannot shine in the shadows of fear. It's with a heavy heart that I announce our pause in pursuing this investigation. We have seen close calls, and threats that have cut too close to our core. This decision is not a step back; it's a strategic withdrawal to protect what we hold dear."

The room seemed to hold its breath as he paused, the silence punctuated by the soft rustle of notepads and the click of cameras. "Our mission is not over. We will reassess, regroup, and redouble our efforts when the time is right. This decision is an investment in the future, ensuring that the truth prevails without further casualties."

His voice softened, sincerity coloring his words, "I understand the disappointment this may evoke, and I assure you it's a decision that wasn't made lightly. We owe it to our colleagues, our families, and our principles to ensure that our pursuit of truth doesn't come at the cost of lives."

With a final nod to the reporters, he concluded, "Thank you for your unwavering support thus far. We remain steadfast in our commitment to exposing the truth, and we will emerge from this hiatus stronger and more determined than ever."

Later that night at Reena's home. The atmosphere was somber as Anderson arrived with James, Lily, and Mark. Reena, John, and Teena were at home, awaiting their arrival. They gathered in the living room, the air thick with tension.

Anderson's face was strained as he looked around the room, his voice heavy with the burden of his decision. "Reena, James, Lily, Mark... I want to look each of you in the eye and tell you that this decision was not made lightly. In my three decades as a journalist, I've faced threats, bribes, and dangers head- on. But for the first time, I find myself taking a step back."

Reena's eyes met Anderson's, her disappointment evident but understanding in her gaze. "Anderson, we've put everything into this investigation. We've faced danger, we've uncovered secrets. To back down now..."

Anderson sighed, his face lined with conflict, "It's not about backing down, Reena. It's about understanding the stakes. You narrowly escaped two close calls. My other staff members weren't as fortunate; they've been targeted with gunshots. I've received warnings, threats... they warned me to be prepared for our lives to be forfeited if we go public."

The gravity of the situation hung heavily in the room. The others exchanged glances, their expressions a mixture of frustration and realization.

Lily's voice was soft as she added her understanding, "It's not just our lives we have to consider. Our families, our loved ones... they're at risk too."

Anderson's gaze remained steady, his voice tinged with emotion. "My wife, Martha, and I had a long and difficult discussion about this. She reminded me of the responsibilities we hold to ourselves and to those who care about us. I realized that I have no right to keep your lives hanging by a thread."

Reena's eyes filled with understanding, although the disappointment lingered. "Anderson, we understand the weight of your decision. We know you're doing what you believe is right."

The room fell into a heavy silence, each person lost in their own thoughts and emotions. The realization of the sacrifices made for the pursuit of truth sank in. In the corner, Teena was already in shock, having listened to the conversation, leaving her with a sense of emptiness.

Anderson drives along a winding road, flanked by towering trees and vast fields. His eyes flicker between the road ahead and the rearview mirror, a troubled expression etched into his face. The car's interior is filled with the hum of tires on asphalt, a lonely sound that resonates with his sense of defeat.

The sudden ring of his phone breaks the monotonous drone. Startled, Anderson glances at the screen, his heart skipping a beat as he sees an unknown number. He answers with a cautious, "Hello?"

The voice on the other end is cold, emotionless. "Great, Anderson. You understood the reality. You gave a good build-up at the press conference. That hype was necessary. Don't attempt to reopen this closed issue. Hand over all your evidence. We'll let you know where to deliver it. Expect our instructions shortly."

Anderson's face turns a shade redder with every word, his knuckles whitening as he grips the steering wheel. He listens, teeth clenched, anger bubbling within him, but he knows he's cornered. The call ends, and the silence of the car becomes a deafening roar. He slams his fist against the dashboard, a futile expression of rage against an unseen enemy.

The story moves to a beach, where the calm waves hold a deceptive beauty as they still roar with intensity. Teena stands by the shore, her feet sinking into the wet sand, her gaze fixed on the horizon. Her eyes are serious, almost haunted, as she contemplates the recent events.

She thinks to herself, "Never expected John to react like that. What a man he is, especially in these times of AI. Loves his wife unconditionally, and never even contemplates another woman in his future. How lucky my sister is... No point in eliminating her. He'd never accept me. Next, Anderson backs down from exposing the scandal. No more life threats to Reena. Even if I were to eliminate her with the faintest hope that John might turn to me, it's risky. If anything goes wrong, escaping the police won't be easy this time. I'd spend the rest of my life in jail. Maybe I should move to New York... But even there, life won't be the same as before. No, I can't. Living in New York would be a constant reminder of my failure. No, Sarah... I would undoubtedly lose my sanity. What's my option now? Is there any foolproof plan left?"

With a heavy sigh, she turns away from the water, her mind still racing. Upon returning home, she sinks into the sofa, lost in thought, whispering to herself with a sense of finality, "No, there's no way to own John."

Her voice is a defeated whisper, a surrender to the realization that her dreams, her plans, and her obsession have all come to naught. The room around her seems to close in, the walls bearing down on her as the truth settles in her heart..

At Reena's home, as the night wraps its embrace around the world, a dimly lit room paints a portrait of unease. Teena lies in bed, her breathing ragged, her body trapped in an invisible struggle. A faint glow from a nearby lamp is the only sentinel in the room. Suddenly, her eyes snap open as if yanked by an unseen force, and she sits up, gasping for breath, her heart pounding against her ribcage like a caged bird.

Her legs, seemingly driven by a force of their own, swing over the edge of the bed and find the floor. She stands, drawn to the small fridge in the corner of the room, an oasis in her desert of fear. The fridge door opens, and she clutches a bottle of water, almost spilling it in her haste. The cool liquid flows down her throat, a balm to her parched soul.

The bottle returns to its place, and Teena takes a deep, steadying breath. Trembling hands run through her hair as she returns to her bed, feeling a smile tugging at her lips. It's as if a weight has lifted, and a new spark has ignited within her. The glow from the lamp seems to dance in her eyes, casting a warm light that highlights a resolve that wasn't there before. She lies down, her mind clear, her heart steady.

As the focus shifts to the world is greeted with a new day. Teena is on the beach, the vastness of the ocean before her, the sand beneath her feet, the wind in her hair. She whispers to a puppy, her voice determined, her eyes shining with a strange fire.

"Listen closely, my dear. I've got a plan."

Chapter 12.

Her fingers gently stroke the puppy's fur as she unfolds her audacious scheme, outlining every detail, every nuance. The puppy's eyes seem to comprehend, fixed on her face as she sketches out her plan in the sand.

"This is Teena, This is John, This is Reena..." she murmurs, drawing the outlines of three figures, her voice filled with a dark thrill. "My brilliant idea is that I will kill Reena with my meticulous criminal brain. Teena [me] is created. John thought Teena had died. The entire world believes Teena Died. In reality, I am alive, and Reena dies. Then John is mine. He never identified the difference between us. We're Exceptional Twins, with the same Height, Weight, handwriting strikes, fingerprints, and even body smell. My little puppy, even you were confused to identify who your boss is and who I am. Excellent..."

Her voice trails off as the sea, like a silent witness, washes away the diagrams. The puppy remains still, its eyes fixed on Teena, a silent participant in her dark dance.

"This is it. My ticket to happiness," Teena whispers to herself, her eyes fixed on the horizon, her mind a whirlwind of thoughts and calculations. The sound of the waves is a constant reminder of the inexorable march of time, and her determination stands tall, a monument to her twisted desires.

Teena awakens a bit later than usual, the tension of the past few days has lifted. A relaxed smile graces her face as she strolls into the living room, her feet padding softly on the floor. The puppy greets her with a wagging tail and the aroma of breakfast wafts from the kitchen where Reena is busy preparing the meal.

John is about to leave for work, but he takes a moment to notice Teena's cheerful expression. With a quick, loving kiss to Reena, he announces his departure, his voice carrying warmth and the familiar note of affection.

In her thoughts, Teena murmurs to herself, "Your next kiss is for me only." A thrill of excitement runs through her, a secret plan taking shape in her mind.

The breakfast call comes soon after, Reena's voice is melodic and inviting. Teena and the puppy move to the dining area, settling into their chairs as the morning sunlight filters through the windows. The meal is enjoyed with pleasant conversation and laughter.

Teena, her voice tinged with a pleasant tone, suggests to Reena, "Let's unwind today, my dear sweetheart. We've been consumed by our worries and forgotten how to relax. How about revisiting our favorite places?" Her eyes sparkle with the idea, and Reena's smile widens in agreement.

Matching dresses, round-neck chains, a journey through cherished spots—the day is planned with delightful enthusiasm.

As the morning turns into the afternoon, the two embark on their adventure. They explore various places, stop for a leisurely lunch, and continue their journey. The car winds through scenic roads, the landscape ever-changing, until they arrive at a trail leading to a hilltop around 4 pm.

The path is scattered with small stones, making it slippery and risky. Every step is filled with care and caution, but the breathtaking view and the cool breeze coax them forward.

Just before they reach the final point, Teena turns to Reena, her eyes twinkling with mischief. "Hey sis, can I borrow your wedding ring for a moment?" she asks playfully.

Reena's eyes narrow with curiosity, but she removes the ring, placing it into Teena's outstretched hand. Teena slides it onto her own finger, promising with a teasing grin, "Don't worry, I promise I'll take good care of it. It's just for a little while."

Reena chuckles, her voice light and teasing, "Well, be careful. That ring belongs to my man, you know."

The banter continues as they reach the edge of the hilltop, both of them captivated by the beauty of nature. The vast expanse of the valley below, the sound of distant birds, and the gentle rustle of leaves—all combine to create a moment of peace and serenity.

Intentionally maintaining a bit of distance from Reena, Teena places the puppy down and moves closer to her sister. Her heart pounds in anticipation as she readies herself to push Reena.

But in an unexpected twist, Teena's foot slips on the wet, slippery ground. She tumbles down into the valley, a scream escaping her lips.

"Teena!" Reena's cry is filled with shock and terror, her eyes wide as she witnesses the unthinkable. The puppy, sensing the distress, tries to peer over the edge as well. The image of Teena's fall lingers in Reena's mind, her scream echoing in the silence. Time seems to freeze, the world holding its breath as the gravity of what just happened sinks in. The puppy's whine, the rustle of the leaves, and the distant sound of a bird are the only reminders that life continues on. Reena's heart pounds in her chest, the shock and disbelief settling into a cold, hard reality. The hilltop, once a place of joy and cherished memories, now stands as a testament to a tragic twist of fate.

Reena sits alone in the car outside the hospital, her eyes vacant and filled with sorrow. Nearby, John enters the hospital building, his steps heavy with grief.

Inside the hospital, in the stark cold of the morgue, he stands beside Teena's lifeless body. The authorities handed him Teena's personal belongings – a chain and a ring. John's eyes linger on the ring, a mix of emotions washing over him.

Outside, John approaches the car where Reena is waiting. He gets in, placing the bag on his lap. Reena's voice is soft and sad as she says, "John, give me the ring..." He looks at her, confusion in his eyes, before reaching into the bag to retrieve the ring. He places it on her finger, and she looks at it, a complex mixture of emotions on her face.

John's voice trembles as he says, "Reena, they gave me Teena's belongings. A chain and this ring..." Reena turn away, unable to meet his eyes. His brows furrow as he picks up the ring, asking, "Why was Teena wearing this ring? Did she explain?"

Reena's voice trembles as she replies, "She asked me to give it to her just before... before she slipped." John's face shifts from confusion to disbelief, struggling as he asks, "She asked you to give her the ring... right before the accident?" Reena nods, tears welling in her eyes.

The weight of the moment hangs heavy as John's voice breaks, "Why? Why would she do that?" Reena's voice cracks as she answers, "I... I don't know, John. It doesn't make sense. She said she wanted to wear it just once..." John's grip tightens on the bag, his thoughts racing, his face a picture of torment.

They sit in the parked car, the silence between them filled with grief and unanswered questions. Finally, the car starts moving, slowly carrying them away from the hospital. The hospital building recedes, but the weight of their grief remains, a heavy burden that neither can shake. The unanswered questions linger, haunting them as they face the road ahead.

As the story draws to a close, their shared grief becomes a poignant reminder of the fragility of life and the complexity of human emotion. The shadows of doubt and uncertainty cast a pall over what should have been a simple farewell, leaving them both to grapple with a mystery that neither can solve. The dialogues resonate in the silence, echoes of a conversation that has changed everything, leaving them with nothing but the aching emptiness of loss.

THE END.

A Note from the Author......Next Page,

Writing this novel has been a labor of love, crafted under challenging circumstances without the basic comforts of food and shelter. If you enjoyed this journey and want to be part of the magic that brings my future projects to life, your support can make a world of difference.

By contributing, you're not just supporting a book, but a dream and the promise of stories yet untold. With your help, here are the titles you can look forward to:

"The Rarest Robbery" "Child Martyrs of Jesus"

"The Best Gift to Your Children" "Except Me"

"Suicide Bomber" "Blind Again"

To extend your support, simply scan the QR code below or paypal.me/csraju85

CS Raju, hailing from India is a versatile writer with a flair for both thrilling narratives and adventurous fantasy tales about pet animals. With a rich background in the film industry, he crafts stories that are ready to leap from the page to the screen. This novel marks his thrilling entry into psychological fiction, showcasing a talent that promises to enthrall readers and filmmakers alike.

CS Raju's work is a testament to creativity, innovation, and the uncharted territories of storytelling.

When identical twins Reena and Teena's lives intertwine with a charismatic model named John, they embark on a dark and twisted journey where love turns to obsession, trust breaks into betrayal, and sisterhood descends into a deadly game.

Reena, the fiery investigative journalist, finds joy and love with John. Teena, the tranquil artist, falls for him in secret, spiraling a desperate quest that leads to shock, violence, and guilt.

The stakes rise as Teena's obsession grows. Her once gentle nature transforms, plotting a terrible fate for her sister. Love and madness dance on a razor's edge, culminating in a shocking twist of fate.

Can love survive betrayal? Can sisterhood endure envy? What price will be paid for unrequited desire? Dive into this gripping psychological thriller and unravel the intricate web of love, deceit, and treachery that binds two identical souls.

OBSESSION
UNLEASHED

Don't miss out!

Visit the website below and you can sign up to receive emails whenever CSRaju publishes a new book. There's no charge and no obligation.

https://books2read.com/r/B-A-CSGAB-MBGOC

BOOKS 2 READ

Connecting independent readers to independent writers.

www.ingramcontent.com/pod-product-compliance
Lightning Source LLC
Chambersburg PA
CBHW031332160726
47993CB00002B/642